TRADEWIND BOOKS

The Heretic's Tomb

Born and raised in Britain, Canadian writer Simon Rose lives in Calgary, Alberta. His first novel, *The Alchemist's Portrait*, was published by Tradewind Books in 2003. *The Sorcerer's Letterbox*, published by Tradewind Books in 2004, was shortlisted for both the Silver Birch and the Diamond Willow awards. His other books for Tradewind Books are *The Clone Conspiracy* (2005) and *The Emerald Curse* (2006).

The Heretic's Tomb

The Heretic's Tomb

by Simon Rose

VANCOUVER   LONDON

Published in Canada and the UK by Tradewind Books Ltd.
www.tradewindbooks.com

Distribution and representation in Canada by Publishers Group Canada
www.pgcbooks.ca

Distribution in the UK by Turnaround
www.turnaround-uk.com

Text copyright © 2007 by Simon Rose
Cover illustration © 2007 by Cynthia Nugent
Book design by Jacqueline Wang

Printed in Canada on 100% ancient forest friendly paper.
10 9 8 7 6 5 4 3 2 1

All rights reserved. No part of this publication may be reproduced, stored
in a retrieval system or transmitted, in any form or by any means, without
prior written permission of the publisher or, in the case of photocopying or
other reprographic copying, a licence from Access Copyright, 75 University
Avenue West, Waterloo, ON Canada N2L 3C5.

The right of Simon Rose to be identified as the author of this work has been
asserted by him in accordance with the Copyright, Design and Patents Act 1988.

Cataloguing-in-Publication Data for this book available from the British Library.

Library and Archives Canada Cataloguing in Publication

Rose, Simon, 1961-
        The heretic's tomb / by Simon Rose.

ISBN 978-1-896580-92-0

        I. Title.

PS8585.O7335H47 2007   jC813'.6   C2007-903779-8

---

*The publisher thanks the Canada
Council for the Arts for its support.*

 Canada Council   Conseil des Arts
for the Arts   du Canada

*The publisher also wishes to thank the Government
of British Columbia for the financial support it
has extended through the book publishing tax credit
program and the British Columbia Arts Council.*

 BRITISH
COLUMBIA
ARTS COUNCIL

*The publisher also acknowledges the financial support of the Government of
Canada through the Book Publishing Industry Development Program (BPIDP)
and the Association for the Export of Canadian Books.*

This book is dedicated to
the memory of Ian Seaton,
lover of history and
devoted husband, father and grandfather.

"When the burning sun is setting,
and your thoughts of care are free.
Whilst of others you are thinking,
will you sometimes think of me."

Sadly missed.

- S.R.

The publisher thanks Mary-Ann Stouck
for her help with the Latin and Middle English.

The author thanks the Alberta Foundation for the Arts
for its financial assistance.

The events and characters depicted in this novel are fictitious. Any similarity to
actual persons, living or dead, is purely coincidental.

contents

Prologue

The Black Death

The first cases of the Black Death in England occurred during the reign of Edward III in the summer of 1348, and the disease spread quickly. By autumn, the plague had reached London, killing nearly half of the city's 70,000 inhabitants. Over the next two years, between thirty and forty percent of the English population, or approximately two million people, died of the plague. In Europe as a whole, it is estimated that at least twenty-five million people died between 1347 and 1351. Outbreaks continued to occur periodically for centuries, and the plague did not disappear from Europe until the eighteenth century.

chapter one

Lady Isabella

Lady Isabella Devereaux watched black plumes of smoke rise from the nearby village of Thornbury. More bodies were being burned. After that fateful day when it struck, the plague killed nearly half the population of England. All across the land, villagers and townsfolk built huge bonfires and dug deep pits to dispose of the ever-increasing number of bodies. The death toll was even higher in London. Isabella's late husband's relatives had sent word of the terrible tide of despair within its walls, only ten miles away. It seemed that no one would be spared the shadow of death that followed the plague's unrelenting path of destruction.

Isabella fingered her silver ring. It contained an amber stone, a reminder of happier times with her family. The terrible disease first took her husband, Sir Robert, then her two young daughters, Mary and Elizabeth. Isabella shuddered as she recalled the morning when she first saw the plague's telltale dark blotches on her husband's skin. Soon after he was buried, her poor daughters were also afflicted with the disease and died. Isabella's entire family had perished and she was alone. Since her home was now filled only with painful memories, Isabella elected to take refuge at nearby Thornbury Abbey, with the encouragement of the abbess, Margaret Bellmare. She'd been offered temporary accommodation with her husband's relatives at the White Swan, their London inn, yet she preferred to stay in the familiar surroundings of her own county.

Sir Edmund Courteney, the local sheriff, offered to look after Isabella's affairs. He arranged for his own men to till her fields and tend to her remaining livestock until she could decide what she wanted to do with her property. Sir

Edmund assured her that she could take as much time as she wished with her decision. Fortunately, Isabella's tenants and retainers had found employment on neighbouring estates and in the village of Thornbury. Because of the heavy death toll, there were labour shortages in every profession.

"Will that be all, my lady?"

Isabella turned to face her last remaining staff, Henry and his wife, Joan. Over the years, Henry had worked as the estate handyman and blacksmith, while Joan had supervised the kitchen. Their meagre possessions were now piled onto a small cart, which stood on the dusty track that led to the village. Earlier that year, they had lost their four children and elderly parents to the plague.

"Yes, thank you, Henry," said Isabella, pressing a few coins into his hand. "God bless you. I know how difficult it has been for you both. I am sorry that I have decided to leave the estate, but at least you will have work as a blacksmith with Sir Edmund. He is a good man and will be sure to look after you."

"Thank you, my lady," said Henry, with a quick bow.

"Now, now," Isabella declared, giving Henry's wife a short hug. "No tears, Joan. You have my deepest gratitude for your faithful service to my family. You have both been so very kind these many years."

Isabella waved to them as their cart disappeared down the road to the village. Then she packed her remaining possessions onto her wagon and gazed one last time at her home.

Just then, two men on horseback galloped up to the house. Isabella recognized the lead figure as Sir Roger de Walsingham, who was closely followed by Fitzwalter, Sir Roger's overseer. A powerful man, Sir Roger owned vast estates in neighbouring counties and was master of the formidable Alversham Castle. He was a seasoned warrior and had fought bravely at King Edward's side during the wars in France, receiving a number of serious wounds. His left hand was missing two fingers, and he had a long deep scar running down the right side of his face. Notorious for the barbaric cruelty he showed to his enemies, he was also rumoured to have poisoned his first wife in order to inherit her considerable land holdings.

Almost immediately after Isabella's husband died, Sir Roger had offered to marry her. But Isabella suspected his motives were far from romantic. She was certain that it was the Devereaux estate that he desired. Although Isabella politely turned down his proposal, Sir Roger would not give up, believing that once her grief had subsided she would change her mind.

Sir Roger approached Isabella's loaded wagon, dressed in his customary black chain mail under a black surcoat that had a white stag embroidered on the chest—the de Walsingham family emblem. His dark hair, beard and black eyes complemented his grim apparel.

Fitzwalter kept his distance. As Isabella examined him from the corner of her eye, she could see why Sir Roger had chosen him as his henchman. Fitzwalter's stocky body was made of pure muscle, and his pale blond hair, icy blue eyes and squat nose made him a frightening presence.

He was extremely loyal and had been in Sir Roger's service for many years, dealing mercilessly with every one of his master's enemies.

"So, my lady," Sir Roger began, "have you reconsidered my proposal?"

As he spoke, his smile accentuated the gruesome scar on his face.

"My lord," Isabella replied, "my answer remains the same. My mind is quite made up."

"But what of your estates and your retainers?"

"My people will be well looked after," Isabella replied, "and Sir Edmund has agreed to administer my estate."

"So it remains your intention to leave?" asked Sir Roger.

"Yes, my lord," Isabella replied. "I have decided to live out my remaining days at the abbey."

A sly grin crept across Sir Roger's face as he removed his chain mail gloves, exposing his deformed hand.

"Surely, it is not your plan to become a nun? A woman of your grace and beauty would be sorely wasted in the service of God."

"As opposed to becoming your wife?" Isabella shot back. "Thereby giving you title to my estate the moment we exchange wedding vows?"

"My lady, consider your situation," he said, calmly stroking his beard with the remaining fingers of his left hand. "Your husband is dead, and you need to remarry. My offer is more than generous. Imagine what your life would be like as Lady Isabella de Walsingham."

"A match with you, my lord, would be a match with the devil himself!" Isabella replied fiercely. "I would rather die!"

Sir Roger's eyes narrowed. He grabbed the whip from his saddle and raised it high in the air.

"You are exceedingly bold," he sneered, "but also most foolish. Mark my words; no one defies Sir Roger de Walsingham! I swear that you will pay dearly for this humiliation!"

Sir Roger turned his horse and galloped away, followed by Fitzwalter. Once she was sure they had gone, Isabella made her way quickly to the safety of her new home at Thornbury Abbey.

chapter two

The Healer
and the Madman

Isabella awoke to the first shafts of morning sunlight streaming down from the windows high up on the wall of her room in the basement at Thornbury Abbey. Living quarters at the abbey were usually quite austere, but Abbess Margaret had allowed Isabella to fix shelves onto the walls for her books, along with the pots, bottles and jars containing the medicines she used in her work. Since her family had passed away, Isabella had devoted her life to tending to the sick and dying. Abbess Margaret praised Isabella for doing the Lord's bidding. She instructed the nuns to harvest whatever herbs and plants Isabella requested to make her medicines. Isabella had soon become a living saint in the eyes of the villagers, and they showered her with affection wherever she went. Isabella herself sincerely believed that God had spared her life so that she might embark on her sacred mission.

Isabella's simple bed and large trunk rested against one wall, and a plain wooden cabinet, which contained more of her medical equipment and supplies, stood beneath the windows. On the top of the cabinet were several bowls, a water jug and a mortar and pestle, which she used to grind and mix herbs and plants to create her remedies.

Isabella got up from the bed and walked over to the cabinet. She picked up the mortar and pestle and sat down at her table. She needed to create more medicines for what would undoubtedly be another busy day. Yet, as she began mixing herbs, she felt overcome by a wave of dreadful despair. She had convinced herself that she was doing the Lord's work and that her very survival had been an act of Divine Providence. And yet, her efforts to save lives always failed. She could treat her patient's symptoms, perhaps even halting the spread of the disease for a night, a day or even a week, but people still died. The plague was unrelenting and was getting worse. However, she felt an obligation to help those who suffered, and with a deep sigh she began preparing medicines for another day.

In the privacy of her room, Isabella wore her hair loose and allowed it to tumble over her shoulders. However, in deference to the nuns at the abbey, whenever Isabella ventured outside her room she always kept her head fully covered in white cloth with only her face showing. After putting the mortar and pestle away, Isabella sat down on her bed and carefully inserted the pins that held her hair in place. Then she covered her head with a white linen wimple. Putting on her cloak, she picked up the saddlebag containing her medicines and slipped the leather strap over her shoulder. Then she stepped out into the darkened hallway, gently closing the door behind her and turning her iron key in the lock.

At the end of a long day attending to plague victims, Isabella came to a cottage belonging to Constance Turner, whose entire family had perished. Isabella had tried to cure her husband and children, but instead had watched them die one by one. Now Constance herself was sick, and Isabella knew she also did not have long to live.

"My lady, why such sorrow?" Constance asked.

"Oh, Constance," sighed Isabella. "I have seen so much death, but I will never grow accustomed to it. And I fear I have failed to save you as well."

Tears began to well in her eyes as she helped Constance swallow what she knew would be her last dose of medicine.

"This will dull the pain and help you to sleep," said Isabella, her voice faltering.

"Do not weep, my lady," said Constance, gasping as she swallowed the potion. "I do not fear death. No one could have done more for me—save perhaps Mad Dominic."

"Mad Dominic?" said Isabella.

"People say Mad Dominic lives alone deep in the forest," Constance replied. "He was once a monk skilled in medicine, rumoured to be the only one in his monastery to survive the pestilence."

Before Isabella could question her further, Constance fell into a deep sleep. With a whispered farewell, Isabella left the cottage. On the journey back to the abbey, Constance's words about the mysterious monk echoed in her mind.

Who knows if Dominic even exists? Isabella thought. *And if he* is *living in the depths of the woods, maybe he really has gone mad.* Nonetheless, she was intrigued and decided to seek out the old man the very next day.

The following morning, Isabella left the abbey and hurried to the forest. Fortunately, it hadn't rained in a few days, so the road that threaded through the centre of the village wasn't the usual damp trench. About a mile outside Thornbury, it connected with the main road to London, only half a day's ride away on horseback.

The low, white-walled houses closest to the

road had roofs made of straw thatch with holes in the middle for the smoke to escape from fire pits inside. Scores of geese wandered freely through the village, and pigs foraged in the mud. Isabella walked past a group of children playing games and noticed that the tavern was already open for business. Women bustled around as they washed clothes and fetched water from the local stream, while men worked in the fields.

The small church with its imposing tower was the focal point of Thornbury village. As she walked by, Isabella nodded to a priest who was chatting with two elderly women in the church doorway. Then Isabella saw two men wearing patched leggings and tunics in vivid blue and green, who were ploughing the field. The ploughman was leading a pair of oxen dragging a heavy blade behind them, while the other man sowed the newly cut furrows with seeds that he carried in a canvas bag slung over his shoulder. Clouds of birds fluttered overhead, swooping down to snatch the seeds before the furrows were covered over.

Isabella followed the twisting dirt track deep into the forest, keeping her right hand close to the concealed dagger attached by a thin chain to the belt around her waist. The woods occasionally served as a hideout for bandits, and she was taking no chances. As she approached a brook, Isabella stopped and scanned her surroundings, wondering where she should start looking for Mad Dominic. She heard the sound of twigs snapping and skirted the edge of the brook in the direction of the noise. Keeping as quiet as possible, she crept through the trees and saw an old man collecting sticks. He had a thick beard and was dressed in filthy rags.

"Dominic!" she called out.

The old man turned around, startled, unsure where the voice had come from. As Isabella stepped out from her hiding place, he yelled at her.

"Begone!" he screeched. "Get away from me!"

Reaching down to the ground, he grabbed a handful of stones and threw them at her.

"Wait!" said Isabella, ducking to avoid the barrage.

The old man turned and disappeared into the forest.

"My name is Isabella Devereaux," she shouted in desperation. "I need your help."

The old man halted and turned to stare at her, his eyes narrowing.

"The healer?" he said.

"Yes," replied Isabella, "or at least that is what some call me."

"And what would you want of me?" he asked.

"I heard that you were once a healer yourself," she replied.

"Come," he said, gesturing with his arm for her to follow him. "This way."

Despite his advanced years, Dominic was surprisingly nimble and could move quickly through the trees. Isabella had trouble keeping up as she scrambled after him through the tangled undergrowth. Eventually, they reached a tiny clearing with a dilapidated old stone cottage in its centre. The roof wasn't made of thatch, but rather constructed from branches and other bits of wood collected over many years. The cottage had only one window, as far as she could tell, and the makeshift door was constructed from three discarded wooden boards, all of different lengths. Isabella watched as the old man walked over to the cottage and sat down on a large log beside the entrance. He gestured for her to join him, but Isabella hesitated.

"Come now," said the old man. "Sit down."

Isabella was taken aback. She had half expected Mad Dominic to be hopelessly insane. But, as the old man patted the log beside him in a gesture of friendship, Isabella's fears quickly melted away.

"Do not be fooled by that Mad Dominic story," the old man said, as if he were reading her mind. "That is only a ruse to help me retain my privacy."

"You are not a lunatic at all, are you?" said Isabella, as she sat down on the log.

"Hardly," the old man chuckled. "I simply like to be alone."

"So why are you prepared to talk to me?" Isabella asked him.

"I have heard your story, Lady Isabella," said Dominic. "I know of the tragedy and heartache that you have suffered and how you seek to help others."

"As did you," Isabella reminded him. "That is why I have sought you out."

"Yes, but after what happened at the monastery," Dominic replied sadly, "*I* have sought only my solitude."

"What happened back there?" asked Isabella.

Dominic took a deep breath.

"The plague arrived utterly without warning," he explained solemnly, "and in our closed religious community, it spread rapidly. I used my medical expertise as best I could, and although I relieved the suffering of some, I was ultimately able to save no one. For some reason, I believed that the Lord had spared me, perhaps to do his work and combat the disease. Yet I was helpless in the face of its onslaught. Eventually I fled. I have lived here ever since."

"I too was spared," declared Isabella. "I also feel that I am fated to devote my life to helping others and yet..."

"And yet you fear there is no hope," said Dominic, nodding. "Yes, it was the same for me, but perhaps I can help you. One moment."

He stood up and went inside the cottage. Sitting alone in the clearing, Isabella couldn't help but appreciate just how peaceful it was here. She had left her own heartache behind to live at the abbey, but could easily understand why Dominic chose to live in isolation in the wilderness.

Her thoughts were interrupted by the screech of a falcon circling in the sky high above. It grew more and more agitated until Dominic emerged from the cottage.

"This may be of great use to you," he said, holding out a battered leather-bound book.

"Aha," he said, gazing up at the circling bird. "I see that she is back." Dominic placed the book on the ground at his feet.

Isabella ducked as the bird swooped down and came to rest on Dominic's forearm. There was a small rabbit clasped tightly in the falcon's talons.

"Before I entered the monastery, I was a falconer," Dominic explained, as he gingerly tugged the rabbit from the bird's grasp. "Cleopatra here was injured, close to death when I found her. I nursed her back to health and trained her. Since then, she has hunted game for me. Perhaps you would care to join me for a meal?"

He produced a small dagger and held up the bloody carcass of the rabbit.

"You are very kind," said Isabella, concealing her distaste, "but please tell me more of this book."

"When I lived at the monastery," Dominic explained, "there was a rumour that the abbot and his most trusted confidants kept a room containing forbidden knowledge of many kinds. When people began to die, the abbot asked me to help and permitted me to use this book. It contains long-forgotten pagan texts from ancient Greece, Rome and the Arab world, describing the remedies to many illnesses. These are purely medical recipes, yet the religious authorities would have frowned on the abbot possessing such a book despite its innocent contents. Hence, he decided to keep it concealed from all but a select few."

"So you used the book to help those suffering at the monastery?" Isabella asked him.

"I tried," said Dominic, "but the plague was too powerful and too fast. Eventually everyone died, including the abbot, and I was left alone, unsure as to why I had survived when all the others had perished. However, before I left the monastery I went to the abbot's secret room and took the book, hoping that I might be able to find a cure if I studied the texts."

"But can these remedies truly cure the plague?" Isabella asked him. "You said yourself that its progress is unstoppable."

"Alas," replied Dominic, shaking his head. "I can make no promises, but the book may at least increase your medical knowledge."

He passed the book to Isabella, but kept his hand over the cover to prevent her from opening it.

"Beware, Lady Isabella," he warned her gravely, "although these are innocent descriptions of how to heal the sick, the book may bring you a swift death sentence if the church authorities ever learn of it. You must always keep the book safely hidden."

After Isabella nodded, Dominic removed his hand from the cover.

"And now," said Dominic, "I am going to roast this rabbit. Do you still not care to join me?"

"No, thank you," Isabella replied. "I must be on my way."

"Farewell, Lady Isabella," said Dominic. "I do hope that we shall meet again."

As she made her way back to the abbey, Isabella was filled with fresh hope. Perhaps she finally had what she needed to fight the dreaded plague.

Chapter Three

The Summons

Back in her room at the abbey, Isabella marvelled at the book Dominic had given her. The book's brown leather covers were decorated with simple tooling, and engravings of roses appeared on each of the four protective metal corners. The volume was held together with two silver clasps, which Isabella carefully unhooked so that she could begin studying the ancient text. Inside was a collection of loose sheets of parchment. The pages were well worn, and some of them had water damage and burn marks. The book was written in Latin, but there were many different styles of handwriting. Some pages also had underlined passages with notes scribbled in the margins, and it was clear that new pages of remedies had been inserted over the years. As Isabella examined the book, she could see that it contained instructions for treating a wide range of ailments, from common chills and fevers to medical conditions she had never even heard of. There were also sections dealing with broken limbs, battlefield wounds and surgery, complete with rudimentary diagrams.

Over the next few weeks, Dominic's book of medical knowledge was invaluable to Isabella. While its remedies proved as ineffectual as her own medicines in combatting the plague, she was able to heal those suffering from other complaints. Isabella's reputation soared, and she found herself travelling ever further afield.

Late one afternoon, while returning to the abbey, she noticed a bird hovering overhead. It made several swoops down close by her head before she realized it was Dominic's falcon, Cleopatra. Isabella stood still, and Cleopatra made several more passes at her before fluttering down and settling on her outstretched forearm. Isabella wasn't sure what to do at first, but then noticed something rolled up around the bird's left leg, tied in place by what looked to be a piece of canvas thread. Cleopatra offered no resistance as Isabella gingerly removed a scrap of old worn parchment with an urgent message from Dominic. *Come quickly. Time is short.*

As Isabella finished reading the note, Cleopatra flew off. Isabella made her way into the forest as quickly as she could and raced through the tangled woods toward the clearing. As she reached Dominic's cottage she saw Cleopatra perched upon the log beside the entrance and noticed that the rickety front door was wide open. Without a moment's hesitation, she went straight into the cottage.

The interior was smaller than she had imagined it to be. The ceiling was so low at the entrance that she had to stoop to avoid colliding with the branches sticking out of the ramshackle roof above. Beneath a hole in the roof a small fire was burning, surrounded by a ring of stones. In the flickering light, Isabella could see that Dominic had almost no furniture, except for a small stool and a low square table. Dominic lay on a wooden bed, beneath several layers of animal fur.

"So Cleopatra managed to find you," Dominic said weakly when he saw Isabella. He began to cough violently.

"Your arm!" exclaimed Isabella.

There were telltale blotches all over the old man's skin.

"Yes," sighed Dominic, "I am dying. It began yesterday, and I sent Cleopatra to seek you out."

"By what means?" Isabella asked.

"I used a spell," Dominic answered.

"Are you a sorcerer?" she demanded, drawing back in horror.

"No, Isabella. But I do have secrets. I have a second book that will help you in your healing mission." Dominic pointed at the far wall. "There is a hiding place in that wall. Remove the loose stone. The book and a mirror are concealed there. Bring them to me."

Isabella did as he asked and brought the ancient book and mirror to Dominic. As he started to speak she sat down on the ground next to his bedside.

"This is no ordinary mirror," said Dominic, running his trembling fingers along the edge of the frame. "With the correct incantation, it is possible to use the mirror to see into the future. I have seen with my own eyes the relentless devastation that the plague will bring. Many more are destined to die."

"From where did you acquire such a marvel?" Isabella asked in amazement.

"I created it myself using this book—the Book of Vorterius," replied Dominic, tapping lightly on the cover of the leather-bound volume Isabella held in her hands.

"Vorterius?" asked Isabella.

"Vorterius's origins are shrouded in mystery. It is rumoured that he was last of a long line of Druid priests, a holy man who could perform great magic. Shortly after he died, over 1000 years ago, his writings were collected and translated by a Roman scholar. This version is only a few hundred years old, I think; no doubt copied secretly by monks to preserve its knowledge."

Isabella opened the book and quickly realized it was like nothing she had ever seen before.

"What spells are these?" she asked, puzzled.

"Unlike the other book," said Dominic, "this is a collection of ancient magic and is totally unrelated to medical matters. When I went to the abbot's secret room to collect the first book I gave you, I also came across this one."

"And I can use these spells to cure people?"

"Not quite. You must first forge the amulet."

"The amulet?" said Isabella, shaking her head. "I do not understand."

"It is all explained in the book," said Dominic, his voice growing fainter. "The amulet will give you the power to conquer death itself."

Dominic began to cough violently and desperately fought for breath.

"It is your only hope," he gasped.

Then Dominic gently closed his eyes and was gone.

Chapter Four

The Book of Vorterius

At the abbey that evening, Isabella made sure that the door to her room was firmly locked before she lifted Dominic's book out of her saddlebag and placed it on the table. Night had fallen, and she used one of her candles to light the cylindrical metal lamp hanging on the wall. Isabella thought about Dominic and wondered if the stones she'd placed over his buried body would be enough to deter the wolves that prowled the forest after dark.

In the candlelight, Isabella could see that this book was similar to the one Dominic had given her earlier, with metal corners and two sturdy clasps. However, the cover of this book had a strange design. In the centre was a metal circle with two snakes intertwined around the edge and the letter 'V' in the middle.

Isabella hesitated to open the book. Even though her family had perished, Isabella believed that God had spared her life in order for her to help others. If she were caught with this book she would surely be condemned as a witch. However, it must have been God's will that she encounter Mad Dominic and receive this ancient volume of spells. The prospect of helping countless people quickly outweighed whatever guilt she had felt for possessing such a forbidden book. She unfastened the cover.

Isabella studied the spells and enchantments well into the night. One chapter contained instructions for creating the mirror that Dominic had given her. One of the many spells granted the ability to speak and understand a foreign language, upon reciting the Latin words *audite ut loqui, dicite ut audire possimus*, meaning *listen that we may talk, speak that we may hear*.

Another useful enchantment could create light in a darkened space with the words *a nocte in lucem*, which Isabella loosely translated as *night to day*. Most of the contents of the book were relatively benign, and there was nothing that would transform Isabella into the world's greatest sorceress. However, she knew that if Abbess Margaret discovered such a heathen work in Isabella's possession, it would mean a death sentence for heresy.

Toward the end of the book there was a chapter devoted to a mysterious amulet. On the page, there were two circular illustrations bearing the design that decorated the book's cover, but with the addition of a small hole at the top. Written on the page were the Latin phrases *mortis victor* and *vitae restitutor*. Isabella quickly translated the words as meaning *conqueror of death* and *restorer of life*. From a cursory reading of the adjacent text, Isabella realized that the function of the amulet was to bring the dead back to life. Her curiosity got the better of her, and as she examined the book in greater detail, her fascination grew. In order to revive a dead person, the amulet was to be placed on the person's chest precisely over the heart, at which point the healer would recite the words: *in nomine Vorterii, mortem expello vitamque restituo* meaning *in the name of Vorterius, I banish death and restore life*. When placed over the heart, the miraculous amulet resurrected a person from the dead, and, at exactly the same time, it would cure the very illness that had previously caused that person's death.

Isabella pulled the mirror out of her saddlebag and stood it up on the table. Then she flipped back through the pages of the book to locate the verse that would activate the mirror.

"Ostende res futuras," she said softly, meaning *reveal the shape of things to come*.

At first nothing happened. Then Isabella stared in astonishment as the mirror rippled and shimmered like the surface of a pond. It then showed Isabella tending to the sick. Just as Isabella began to wonder about the abbess, the images in the mirror suddenly switched to Abbess Margaret walking in the cloister upstairs. Isabella suspected that the mirror was linked to her own thoughts. When she asked herself how the terrible disease might develop in the months to come, the mirror changed again. As the images of death and despair flashed before her eyes, it became clear to her that the disease would be a threat for decades to come. Despite the risk to her own life, Isabella decided to create the amulet.

She carefully studied the instructions in the book. The amulet had to be silver and had to be made whole but then cut into two halves. The halves then needed to be secured together by an iron clasp in order for it to function. This was meant as a safeguard to ensure that someone wishing to use the amulet for evil could not easily access its power. Isabella had a small collection of silver spoons that she had brought to the abbey from her home, but realized that she would need a blacksmith to forge the amulet. She decided to bring the design to her former blacksmith, Henry, who now worked on Sir Edmund Courteney's estate. Isabella was sure she could trust him and resolved to go and see him the very next day.

When she awoke, Isabella decided it would be too dangerous to take the Book of Vorterius with her. So before she set out to see Henry, she carefully removed the page with the amulet diagrams and put it inside her saddlebag.

When she arrived at Sir Edmund's stable, Henry was working at his anvil hammering a set of horseshoes. Coals glowed white-hot in the furnace.

"My lady!" Henry uttered in surprise. "What brings you here?"

"A favour, Henry," replied Isabella, taking the parchment and spoons from her saddlebag. "If you melt down these silver spoons, could you forge this?"

She handed him the amulet diagram.

Henry carefully studied the illustrations. "Yes, my lady," he said, mopping his brow. "It is a simple design."

"When could you have it finished?" Isabella asked him.

"I will need to make a mould," he replied, "but could probably have the object ready for you by sunset. What is it exactly, my lady?"

"It is a gift for the abbess," Isabella lied, "on the occasion of the fifth anniversary of her arrival at Thornbury, hence the Latin letter 'v', symbolizing five."

Fortunately, Henry accepted this explanation without question. He was a little skeptical when Isabella asked him to split the amulet into two halves and fasten them together with an iron clasp. However, Isabella convinced him that this was just something decorative.

Isabella spent the day tending to the sick and returned to collect the amulet from Henry just before sunset. That evening at the abbey, she reinserted the parchment illustrating the amulet back into the book. Yet as she did so, she decided to hide the two pages that contained the instructions for creating the amulet, as well as the incantation to activate it. If by some chance the amulet ever fell into the hands of a person of less virtue, they would not be able to use its power.

After carefully removing the two pages from the book, Isabella held them up to the candle and read the incantation over and over again. But suddenly the parchment caught fire and swiftly disintegrated into ashes before her eyes. Isabella was in shock. But thankfully she had memorized the verse. She comforted herself with the knowledge that without the incantation no one with evil intent would ever be able to use the amulet.

chapter five

The Amulet's Power

The following morning, Isabella was shocked when Abbess Margaret informed her of the death of Lady Katherine Courteney and her son and two daughters. Sir Edmund Courteney had been administering Isabella's lands since she began living at the abbey. Courteney's own estate had been ravaged by the plague, and along with his wife and children, many of his tenants had also perished. The abbess handed Isabella a letter from Sir Edmund, summoning her to his estate. Although he knew that there was little hope, Sir Edmund had faith that Isabella could offer some much needed comfort to his surviving loyal retainers in their final hours.

Sir Edmund Courteney was a tall, bearded man with light-brown hair. His family had been granted an estate after the Norman Conquest in 1066, and his ancestors had always been loyal to the Crown. Like his father and grandfather before him, Courteney held the rank of sheriff.

"Lady Isabella," said Courteney, his voice quivering and his face ashen as he greeted her. "Thank you for coming. I know how many demands there are on your time."

Isabella placed her hand reassuringly on his arm. "My sympathies are with you at this distressing time. How may I be of service?"

A young boy approached and stood at Courteney's side. He was around twelve years old, slender and quite tall for his age, with sparkling blue eyes and a head of thick black hair.

"Lady Isabella," Courteney announced, "this is Will, the son of my late groom. His parents, sister and brother have all passed away from the pestilence."

"I am so sorry," said Isabella, struggling to hold back her tears as she thought of her own lost family.

"Remarkably," Courteney continued, "Will has not been affected by the disease. I have heard of those who are seemingly immune, but no one knows exactly why the plague spares some but not others. Will has been helping remove the bodies, as he seems very unlikely to contract the plague himself. He has also been able to tend to the sick, helping with their meals and delivering some of the medicine. He has even taught himself to read, and I must admit that he has become quite skilled in medical matters, have you not, Will?"

"Yes, my lord," the boy replied.

"Perhaps you would like some help today, as you tend to the sick?"

"You are most gracious, Sir Edmund," Isabella replied with a smile. "I would be glad of the company and the assistance. Where shall we begin?"

"Perhaps with the people in the cottages closest to the stream?" Courteney suggested. "Will can show you the way."

Will nodded and Isabella followed him down the pathway.

As Isabella treated her first patient, Will became curious about her healing practices.

"Do you not consult the stars, my lady?" he asked with a puzzled look.

"This disease has little to do with the heavens, Will," replied Isabella as she mopped the brow of a teenage girl.

She instructed Will to add some water to a powdered concoction of herbs and the roots of medicinal plants.

"But the doctors who have visited before have always referred to their astrological charts," said Will, as he helped the young girl to swallow the liquid.

"That is not my way, Will. I practise medicine, not magic."

Isabella applied what remedies she could to ease the suffering of Sir Edmund's tenants. Will was a great help, and his aptitude for healing work deeply impressed Isabella.

"Where did you learn about medicine?" Isabella asked him as they left the last cottage.

"When my family died, Sir Edmund took me under his wing," Will told her. "I was able to learn about healing from one of his books. I also assisted some other physicians at work when they visited. But none of them worked as you do."

"Pray tell," said Isabella. "What did they do?"

"Bleeding mostly," replied Will, "but they also employed strange potions made from animal dung, the hooves of wild boars and powdered stags' antlers."

"And did any of those things work?" Isabella asked.

Will shook his head.

"No, my lady. The poor unfortunates only seemed to die all the more quickly."

"Would you like to work with me again, Will?" Isabella asked. "Your assistance has been invaluable today, and I would be most grateful for an apprentice."

"It would be an honour, my lady," Will replied, "but I fear Sir Edmund needs me here."

When they returned to the manor house, however, Courteney was delighted and readily gave his permission for Will to work with Isabella. He also promised that he would send money periodically to help pay for Will's upkeep and accommodation.

From that day on, Will began living at Thornbury Abbey as Isabella's apprentice. Isabella thought of Will as the son she had never had and as a replacement for the daughters she had lost. Will, in turn, came to view Isabella as his second mother.

Once Isabella felt that Will was ready, she showed him the Book of Vorterius and the mirror Dominic had given her. Will was fascinated, and Isabella began teaching him as much Latin as he could absorb, explaining to him what she knew of the spells in the book, the amulet and how the mirror worked.

One day, Isabella and Will were summoned to Sir Roger de Walsingham's estate to tend to the sick. Isabella was apprehensive about seeing Sir Roger again. Yet she had accepted that her mission to help the suffering must always take priority. When she arrived, she was relieved to learn that Sir Roger was away.

After doing what they could to help the plague victims, Isabella and Will began their journey home. As they were riding down the pathway, Will suddenly became very pale. Isabella immediately noticed a few dark blotches on his skin and realized that there was very little time. She brought their horse to a halt outside an abandoned cottage. Isabella then helped Will inside and lay him down on the straw bed.

"My lady," said Will, his voice almost a whisper, "it is too late for me."

"No, Will," Isabella retorted, struggling to control her emotions. "Let me make you comfortable. I have something for the pain."

Isabella searched in her saddlebag, pulling out some medicine. Yet before she could administer it, Will was already dead. Tears streamed down Isabella's face. The pain in her heart was so intense she could not bear it. She had lost one family to the sickness already, and now the only other person she had come to love was gone as well. She cried and cursed the plague, until she remembered the amulet she now possessed. Isabella knew that it would be risky to use the amulet, but the thought of burying Will was unbearable. She began searching for the two halves of the amulet in the bottom of her saddlebag. Taking them out, she carefully manoeuvred the iron clasp into place and fastened it tightly. Isabella then gently placed the amulet on Will's chest, directly over his heart, and spoke the forbidden verse from the Book of Vorterius.

"In nomine Vorterii, mortem expello vitamque restituo."

At first nothing happened, and Will's body remained cold. Then, slowly, the amulet began to glow pale green. Will's eyelids flickered, and he began to cough. She could see that he was disoriented, and helped him sit up. The dark blotches on his skin had faded away without a trace. It was truly a miracle, and she hugged Will as tightly as she could.

"How very touching," said a voice behind her.

Isabella turned her head and to her horror saw Sir Roger de Walsingham standing in the open doorway.

"My lord," said Isabella, struggling to regain her composure as she quickly shoved the amulet back into her saddlebag. "I was not aware that you had returned."

"No doubt," said Sir Roger, with a cruel smile. "It is highly unlikely that you would attend to my tenants if you knew that you might encounter me."

"My lord," Isabella replied, collecting her medicines. "I would have come whatever the cost. It is my sacred duty to administer to the sick."

"Ah yes," sneered Sir Roger, "for which you declined my offer to become Lady de Walsingham." He stroked his beard thoughtfully. "And what ails your assistant?"

"A chill, nothing more," said Isabella. She helped Will to his feet and prepared to leave.

"I think not," Sir Roger countered. "He appeared to be at the very point of death." Then he added with a sneer, "Have you managed to defeat the pestilence?"

"Alas, my lord," Isabella responded, "my efforts only serve to ease the suffering of the sick. The plague is too powerful for my humble remedies."

With her arm around Will's shoulder, she walked toward the doorway.

"And what of the object you used to help your young friend?" asked Sir Roger, barring the exit.

"Object, my lord?" Isabella said innocently. "I know of no object."

"Do not play games with me," he snarled. "The boy was close to death, maybe even dead. I heard your heretical incantation. What sorcery are you engaged in?"

"I am a woman of God," Isabella retorted, "on a sacred mission."

"Perhaps Abbess Margaret would be interested to know about the incantation you spoke."

"I know nothing of such matters," Isabella snapped. "Let us pass."

Sir Roger hesitated, then stepped aside. He watched from the doorway as Isabella and Will climbed onto their horse. As they rode away, the sly grin on Sir Roger's face made Isabella feel very uneasy.

chapter six

Sir Roger's Revenge

"May I remind you, my lord," said Abbess Margaret as she refilled Sir Roger de Walsingham's wine goblet, "that Lady Isabella is viewed as a saint in the local community. At this very moment, she is tending to the sick. The people believe she possesses a gift from God."

Abbess Margaret was a plump, middle-aged woman. Her hair and head were completely covered, revealing only her round face. She wore exquisitely decorated dark robes, a thick golden necklace and jewelled rings on most of her fingers. Sir Roger had arrived at Thornbury Abbey earlier that morning, demanding to see the abbess on a matter of urgency. Abbess Margaret was about to begin mass, but knew that it was unwise to keep a man like Sir Roger waiting in the cloister. After calling for some food and wine, she returned to her private quarters, where Sir Roger joined her.

"I too have heard such tales," Sir Roger nodded, then added darkly, "but I have also heard rumours that Lady Isabella is engaged in heresy."

"Surely you can see that she is engaged in the Lord's work," replied the abbess. "He has explicitly spared her from the ravages of the pestilence so that she may help others."

"Perhaps Lady Isabella's survival is due to other factors," Sir Roger suggested, taking a sip of his wine.

"What are you implying?" asked the abbess.

"Some people believe that she is actually responsible for bringing the plague to their villages," Sir Roger continued. "Some people even believe that she may, in fact, be in the devil's employ."

"Nonsense," exclaimed the abbess. "I have seen her care and compassion with my own eyes."

"And have you also seen what she keeps in her room here at the abbey?" Sir Roger asked her.

"My lord, I respect the privacy of those who are not nuns who take refuge here," Abbess Margaret replied. "Lady Isabella is not bound by the same rules as those who have taken holy orders."

"But surely it would be wise to examine her lodgings, if only to put any gossip to rest? You have a separate key, do you not, to all the rooms here at the abbey?"

Sir Roger gestured toward the wall behind Abbess Margaret, where scores of keys, large and small, hung on hooks.

"I could not in good conscience violate her room, my lord," said the abbess, shaking her head.

"As you wish," said Sir Roger, draining his goblet. "I am sure that the bishop will be very interested to learn that a heretic is living in your abbey."

"But my lord," began the abbess, "I never said—"

"A simple examination of her room is all I require," he interrupted. "Lady Isabella will never know anyone has been in her lodgings, and you will not be held to blame."

Reluctantly, Abbess Margaret took one of the keys from the wall and made her way down to Isabella's chamber, with Sir Roger following closely behind her.

Abbess Margaret lingered in the doorway as Sir Roger entered Isabella's room. It was still only mid morning and the sunlight beaming through the high windows was more than sufficient for them to look around.

"Everything appears to be in order," the abbess remarked.

"Perhaps, but we must look more closely," Sir Roger replied.

A solitary table displayed a small upright mirror in a frame, flanked by a pair of silver candleholders. Two beds, one large and one small, rested along one wall. Sir Roger immediately noticed the large trunk, but when he opened it and rummaged through its contents, he found nothing but clothes. As he examined the shelves he took care in replacing every book, pot, bottle and jar exactly as he had found them, but he was unable to locate the elusive object that he sought. He then turned his attention to the wooden cabinet beneath the windows. But when he opened the doors, he saw that it contained only medical equipment and supplies.

Sir Roger cursed himself for being so naive. It was most likely that Isabella carried the object with her. He gently closed the cabinet doors and turned his attention to the items on top. When he picked up one of the bowls, the small pestle inside it fell to the floor. As he stooped to pick it up he noticed something lodged beneath the larger bed. Reaching in, he pulled out two leather-bound books. As he knelt on the floor he carefully opened the first volume. Sir Roger could easily see that it contained instructions for medical remedies.

The cover of the second book depicted two snakes intertwined around the edge of a circle with the letter 'V' in the centre. With trembling fingers, Sir Roger opened it and was astonished at what he saw. Flipping through the pages, he immediately knew what it was about—powerful magic. If only he could show the book to Skerne, his personal alchemist. Skerne would know exactly what kind of devilry the book contained. He carefully replaced the volume of medical remedies under the bed and stood up, clutching the other book to his chest. He turned around and held the book up for Abbess Margaret to see.

"That book," she gasped in horror as she stared at the image on the cover, "is it ..."

"I fear so," Sir Roger said, gravely. "It is devoted to the dark arts. Lady Isabella is indeed engaged in the devil's work."

"We must inform the bishop immediately," the abbess insisted.

"Indeed we must," agreed Sir Roger. "I intend to take this book to him right away. Such heresy must be dealt with swiftly. I must ask, however, that you keep this matter between us until I have had time to inform His Grace. You know how quickly word can spread. It could give Lady Isabella a chance to flee. If she returns to the abbey, ensure that you act as if nothing has happened."

Abbess Margaret nodded, and Sir Roger left the room, clutching the Book of Vorterius close to his chest.

Rather than riding directly to the bishop's palace, Sir Roger hurried to his own fortified castle at Alversham, where Skerne was waiting. Located in the depths of the fortress, Skerne's laboratory was a dark, dungeon-like room. There was little furniture apart from a large wooden table in the centre of the laboratory and smaller tables against two of the walls. Scientific equipment lay scattered about, and the shelves on the walls were filled with jars of coloured liquids and powders, as well as many large books and scrolls. The room was illuminated by several flaming torches attached to the walls. Opposite the doorway was a large fireplace, beside which hung bellows, tongs and an assortment of blacksmith's tools.

"Skerne," Sir Roger called out as he burst through the door.

The stooped figure standing beside the hearth coughed and spat into the fire, then turned around to reveal a middle-aged man with shoulder length, straggly grey hair. He had a long thin face and a slender nose, and his smile revealed his numerous missing teeth. When he moved it was clear that he had a pronounced limp.

"Take a look at this," said Sir Roger. He crossed over to the fireplace and handed Skerne the Book of Vorterius.

"Where did you get it?" Skerne asked, as he ran his bony fingers over the book's cover.

"In the lodgings of Lady Isabella Devereaux at Thornbury Abbey," Sir Roger replied.

He then explained how he'd heard Isabella reciting Latin incantations when he'd encountered her and Will on his estate.

"I had heard rumours that such a book might exist," Skerne murmured, flipping through the pages, "but I had no idea that they were true. Why, with the spells in this book, a man could—"

"She had an object with her," Sir Roger interrupted him, "an amulet or a medallion, perhaps. The boy was dead, I am sure of it. She used the object to bring him back to life. Is there something in this book that could create such an item?"

"It is possible," said Skerne.

He flipped through the sheets of parchment, arriving at the page with illustrations of the amulet's two halves.

"There are some pages missing," Skerne said. "But look at the words that are written here, *mortis victor* and *vitae restitutor*."

"Conqueror of death, restorer of life," said Sir Roger. "This is a powerful object indeed, and one that I must possess. I shall use the amulet to raise the dead."

"Raise the dead?" Skerne repeated, looking puzzled.

"Look around you," Sir Roger continued. "The pestilence continues with no hope in sight. The Lord has deserted this place. Even the king has abandoned us! I say we need a new king."

"A man such as yourself, my lord?" inquired Skerne.

"It is not without precedent," Sir Roger replied. "I am sure that you remember what happened to the king's late father?"

"Indeed," confirmed Skerne, with a devilish grin, "a most ghastly fate befell the second King Edward to rule this island."

"And the third one deserves no less," Sir Roger growled. "My brother, Sir Hugh, would still be alive today if it were not for the king's treachery on the bloody battlefield of Crécy three years ago. He would never have perished had the king sent in reinforcements as my brother requested."

"But my lord," Skerne reminded him, "your plans have been so carefully thought out. Your men are ready to move at your command, and your fellow conspirators await your signal."

"That is true," Sir Roger agreed. "Yet to ensure success, I will need overwhelming numbers. If I can revive an army of dead soldiers we could overthrow the king and take the crown."

"Then, my lord," Skerne assured him, with a grin, "I shall do my utmost to ensure that you have the means to raise such an unholy force."

"Be sure that you do," warned Sir Roger. "Study the book well. In the meantime, I shall visit Lady Isabella Devereaux. Fitzwalter!"

The sound of footsteps echoed in the hall.

"Yes, my lord," Fitzwalter replied, as he stood in the doorway.

"Saddle the horses," Sir Roger ordered. "We must leave at once."

chapter seven

The Accused

It was late in the afternoon when Isabella and Will returned to Thornbury Abbey.

"Someone has been in my room," she said.

"How can you tell?" Will asked. "Everything looks the same."

"Not quite," said Isabella, pointing to the pestle lying on the floor beside the cabinet.

"The books!" she cried. Dropping to her knees, she fumbled frantically under the bed. The only book she found was Dominic's volume of medical remedies.

"The Book of Vorterius is gone," she said, grimly. "Sir Roger de Walsingham must have taken it."

"How can you be sure it was him?" Will asked her.

"I cannot," said Isabella, smiling, "but the mirror will reveal the truth."

She sat down at the table with Will standing beside her and recited the verse *ostende res futuras*. The mirror misted over, and when it cleared, Isabella and Will watched Sir Roger kneeling on the ground, poring over the pages of the Book of Vorterius. Abbess Margaret stood in the doorway behind him.

Isabella's worst fears had come to pass. She realized with horror that Sir Roger now had what he needed to seal her doom. No doubt Abbess Margaret, her former ally, would turn against her. The scene in the mirror then changed, and they saw Sir Roger handing the Book of Vorterius to Skerne in his laboratory.

Isabella abruptly pulled the top of the frame toward her and lay the mirror face down on the table.

"It is no longer safe here. Both our lives are in danger."

Isabella stood up and took the amulet from her saddlebag. She placed one half, along with the iron clasp, underneath a floor tile in the corner of the room and pressed the other section into Will's hand.

"Keep it secret," she said softly.

"But I want to stay with you," Will protested. "I am not afraid of Sir Roger de Walsingham. I can help."

"No, Will," said Isabella. "Sir Roger is too powerful. If he has the book, then his plans for my demise will have already been put into motion. He has already shown the book to the abbess and will no doubt take it to the bishop to have me condemned as a heretic. You must flee while you still can."

"But—" Will began.

"Not another word," Isabella interrupted, putting her finger to Will's lips. "You must go to London. There is an inn there called the White Swan, which is run by relatives of my late husband. If you mention my name to them you will be welcomed and treated well."

"But what about you?" Will asked, anxiously.

"Have no fear. I will join you in London," Isabella assured him. "Now go, before it is too late. You must make a good start before nightfall."

Isabella gave Will a final hug and a kiss on the cheek. As he left the room, she struggled to control her tears, wondering if she would ever see him again. Then she closed the door and frantically began gathering a few of her possessions. But before she could escape, the door burst open. It was Sir Roger and Fitzwalter.

"Stand guard," Sir Roger ordered.

Fitzwalter nodded and stood like a statue outside the doorway.

Sir Roger advanced slowly into the room.

"So, my lady," he said, "it would appear that your time has run out. I have your book of witch's spells, a book the abbess found most disturbing. I am sure that the bishop will too, but there is no need to tell him, at least not yet. Perhaps we can conduct a little trade? Your life for something of similar value, perhaps?"

Isabella remained silent. She knew that the Book of Vorterius alone was enough to condemn her to death.

"I will not play games," Sir Roger continued. "I wish to have the amulet that you used to revive your assistant on my estate."

"The object you saw at the cottage was a harmless trinket," Isabella lied. "An old family heirloom, that is all."

"Do you take me for a fool, my lady?" roared Sir Roger. "I understand its power and I will possess it! Now give it to me!"

"I no longer have it," said Isabella. "The amulet is lost forever."

"You lie!" Sir Roger snarled.

"No, my lord," Isabella shot back, "it is the truth. The amulet does indeed have the power to conquer death. But I made a vow to never let it fall into the hands of those who might use it for evil. On my way back to the abbey, I threw it in the river."

"Lies and more lies!" screamed Sir Roger, who proceeded to tear the room apart.

He upturned both beds and ran his arm over the shelves, shattering many of Isabella's jars on the floor. He kicked the cabinet repeatedly until it was nothing more than a heap of splinters.

"The flames and the stake are too lenient for a witch like you," he sneered, advancing steadily toward Isabella, who backed away toward the door. "We should consider something slower. Perhaps I will wall you up to die of starvation."

Isabella continued backing toward the door until she bumped up against Fitzwalter behind her. As she did so, Sir Roger grinned widely and nodded. Suddenly, Fitzwalter's arms were wrapped around Isabella, restraining her. She tried to scream, but Sir Roger produced a bottle from his pocket and removed its cork. He quickly poured the contents onto a small cloth and held it over Isabella's nose and mouth. She struggled. But it was no use, and she slipped into unconsciousness.

When she awoke, Isabella found herself lying on her bed. Raising her hands to her head, she realized that her hair had been shorn, in accordance with the law regarding heretics. Still groggy, Isabella struggled to sit up and at first couldn't believe what she saw. The wooden door to her room had been removed and replaced by a solid wall of bricks. She cursed Sir Roger as she staggered over to where the doorway had been. She was hopelessly trapped. Some of her shelves were empty and others had been brutally pulled from the walls. Her books, including Dominic's volume of medical remedies, were nowhere to be seen. Sir Roger had also removed Will's bed, but he had neglected to take the trunk. Broken pottery lay all over the floor. Only the jug, a few pots and a mixing bowl were still in one piece. All the medicines were gone.

Isabella wondered if Will had escaped. Thankfully the floor tile that concealed the amulet had been left undisturbed. She shuffled over to the corner of the room and was about to reach down, when a noise made her turn around. One of the bricks in the former doorway was being removed. Sir Roger peered at her from the other side.

"As you can see, my lady," he said, "I am a man of my word. You are quite alone now. No one can save you. Simply tell me where the amulet is, and I will spare your life."

"I already told you," Isabella insisted. "It is gone forever. It can never be yours."

"As you wish," Sir Roger growled. "Perhaps you will reconsider after several days without food and water."

After he replaced the brick, Isabella heard him stalk off down the hallway.

Chapter Eight

The White Swan

The White Swan, a long-established inn, was located on a busy side street close to London Bridge. Branches and leaves had been nailed over the front entrance to let passers-by know that wine could be purchased inside. The inn offered lodging for travellers all year round but was busier in the summer and on market days. It was a popular establishment, with a substantial cellar.

Will enjoyed his new job as stable boy at the inn, but today, while he was grooming the horses, his thoughts drifted back to Lady Isabella. He'd wanted to stay and help her defend herself against Sir Roger, but she insisted that he flee. Will dragged a coarse brush across the coat of one of the stable horses. He softly patted the animal on its side to calm it down a little. The horses in the other stalls were all quietly eating their hay.

Both Will's father and grandfather had looked after the Courteney family's horses, and as soon as Will was old enough, he had learned the trade. He had spent his entire life on the Courteney estate, and aside from his short time with Isabella, he had never lived anywhere else. The Courteney estate had been a happy place until the plague swept through and claimed Lady Katherine and her children.

Will had considered going to Sir Edmund for refuge, rather than fleeing to London. However, he was uncertain whether Courteney would welcome him. If Isabella were to be convicted of heresy, then Sir Edmund would certainly not shelter him. He had similar concerns when he arrived at the White Swan. Although Isabella had assured him that her relatives would welcome him, Will erred on the side of caution when he introduced himself to the innkeeper and his family. Will cared deeply for Isabella, but since she had promised to join him in London, he decided to keep a low profile until she arrived. He told the innkeeper his name was John Graves and intentionally neglected to mention anything about Lady Isabella Devereaux.

Will finished grooming the horse and put the brushes away in a wooden box next to the stall. That morning, he was supposed to go to the market to collect some fruit and vegetables for the innkeeper's wife. He reached into his tunic and pulled out the half amulet that Isabella had given to him for safekeeping. Will knew that if he was ever found with it on his person it could mean a death sentence. Consequently, whenever he left the inn, he always hid the amulet in a shallow hole he had dug underneath the horses' feeding trough.

Waiting until a small herd of cattle had passed by the inn on their way to the livestock market at Smithfield, Will grabbed a basket in which to carry the fruit and vegetables and stepped out into the busy street. When he heard a noise from above him, he quickly pulled back into the stable entrance. A woman on the second floor was emptying a bucket out of the window in the general direction of the open drainage channel that ran down the centre of the thoroughfare.

Once the coast was clear, Will made his way through the narrow meandering streets, past the closely-packed half-timbered and whitewashed buildings. Most of the houses were two stories high, but the second floor always overhung, with the result that very little sunlight reached street level. On the ground floor there were shops, run by carpenters, butchers, tailors and other vendors, that encroached onto the street, making the busy, crowded lane even more narrow and congested. There were many stables like the one at the inn, with dung heaps piled high in the adjacent alleys. Dozens of pigs wandered back and forth, adding to the foul smells that bombarded Will as he went on his way.

Finally, Will reached the marketplace, located in a square flanked by warehouses, stables and shops, and paved with uneven cobblestones. Despite the heavy toll the plague had taken on the city, the market was a noisy bustling hive of activity. Men and women wandered along the narrow aisles between the covered wooden stalls, negotiating prices, stopping to examine food or simply gossiping with friends and acquaintances. Merchants cried out the names and prices of their goods and products, attempting to drown out the voices of their competitors. Weaving his way through the teeming crowds, Will quickly purchased the fruit and vegetables and started to make his way back to the White Swan. At the edge of the marketplace he overheard two men talking on some stone steps.

"A witch, you say?" said a red-haired man.

"Aye," his bald-headed friend replied, "at Thornbury Abbey. I heard it from a farmer yesterday. Lady Isabella something, I forget the last name. She lived at the abbey in one of the dungeons, they say. The pestilence did not even affect her village, but she went around pretending to be a healer while she was actually giving people the plague."

"It is truly the devil's work," agreed the red-haired man, nodding.

"What happened to her?" Will asked, attempting to join the conversation.

"Dead, I expect," said the bald man, "and good riddance too. The farmer said that she was to be burned at the stake but that the abbess feared she would use her magic to escape the flames. It seems they walled her up in her room instead and left her to starve to death." The man paused as he scratched at his beard, then added, "I heard that she had an accomplice."

"Really?" said Will, feeling decidedly uneasy.

"Yes, a young boy around your age, I heard," the man continued. "They say he helped her cast the spells that gave people the disease. Only a child of course, but possibly even more dangerous than her."

"Is the boy dead too?" Will asked.

"He fled," replied the man, "but he's sure to be found."

"You seem very interested in this witch," said the red-haired man, getting to his feet. "What did you say your name was? I have never seen you around the market before."

"That is true," the bald man agreed. He moved his hand to the dagger that hung from his waist. "They said that the witch's boy was tall and slim, with thick black hair, just like you."

Will struggled to stay calm.

"This is only my second day at the market," he answered. "My parents both died last week of the plague."

The two men didn't appear entirely convinced by his answer. But before they could act upon their suspicions, Will slipped away into the crowd and sprinted back to the inn as fast as he could.

Back in the stables at the White Swan, Will removed the amulet from its hiding place and held it in his hands, recalling how Isabella had placed it there before he fled to London. She had saved his life, and Will knew that no matter what the danger, he had to return to Thornbury Abbey to try to rescue her.

Chapter Nine

Mirror Mirror

Sir Roger de Walsingham grinned widely as he once again read the warrant for the execution of the convicted heretic, Lady Isabella Devereaux of Thornbury Abbey. Earlier that morning, he had made a final attempt to convince the arrogant witch to give up the amulet, or at least to reveal its true whereabouts, but she had again refused and spurned his offer to save her life. Sir Roger had finally lost patience and left her in the room to die.

As he waited in the cloister for Abbess Margaret to meet him, he examined the document once more. He marvelled at how Skerne had so expertly replicated the bishop's handwriting and signature, with which the abbess was very familiar. The warrant also bore the bishop's seal, or rather it had been stamped with a duplicate of the official insignia, also fabricated by Skerne the day before. When Abbess Margaret finally appeared, Sir Roger handed her the scroll, confident that she would be convinced of the warrant's authenticity.

"Well, Sir Roger," the abbess said after she had finished reading, "everything appears to be in order, although I must admit this is all rather irregular."

"The punishment is somewhat unusual," Sir Roger agreed, "but the bishop has given his consent to death by starvation. The wall ensures that Lady Isabella cannot escape, although we cannot be certain of what satanic powers she may still possess."

"Is she completely secure in her lodgings," asked the abbess, with a look of concern, "or would you recommend posting guards?"

"Come with me," Sir Roger assured her. "I will show you that you have nothing to fear."

Together they walked down to Isabella's chambers, where Fitzwalter was waiting.

"Behold," Sir Roger said as he tapped on the mortar, "the wall is as solid as rock. Be sure the entire lower level is kept off limits until the witch is dead."

Abbess Margaret bade him farewell. Once she was gone, Sir Roger took the brick out of the wall to check on Isabella one last time.

"You see, Fitzwalter. She is almost dead."

Isabella was weak with hunger and drifted in and out of consciousness. Through the hole in the wall she could hear Sir Roger confiding in his henchman.

"We must continue our search for the boy," Sir Roger said. "Perhaps he has the amulet I seek."

Isabella remained on the bed as she heard them replace the brick into the wall. She waited until she was certain they had left the lower level, then quietly shuffled over to the table. She had to know that Will was safe. Scarcely able to stand, she collapsed into the chair and stared into the mirror. She gasped at the sight of her pitiful condition. Her once beautiful long blond hair was now short like a man's, emphasizing her long thin neck. Her skin was ashen, her formerly bright blue eyes were faded, and her pale cheeks were sunken.

Isabella softly spoke the Latin words to activate the mirror, and as the image came into focus she saw the busy streets of London. She strained her eyes, fiercely determined to see if she could pick out Will's face in the crowds. Almost immediately, the mirror flashed to the White Swan. Isabella breathed a sigh of relief when she saw Will standing outside the inn's stable, tending to one of the guest's horses. Then, oddly, the scene in the mirror altered, and Isabella saw a young girl in strange clothes, wandering around a ruined landscape surrounded by a number of tall slim structures. To Isabella, they resembled the scaffolding towers she had seen used in the construction of churches, but these towers were not wooden and were much, much taller. In the background, she saw a church with a tall spire and bizarre, brightly coloured carriages speeding back and forth, but with no horses to pull them. As the picture changed again, the same young girl appeared to be standing in Isabella's lodgings at the abbey, but the room looked completely different and was covered in dust. Before she could make sense of what she was seeing, Isabella's vision grew blurred, and she collapsed sideways off the chair. Her outstretched arm upset the mirror, and it shattered on the cold stone floor.

The Present Day

Chapter Ten

Uncovering the Past

Finally the hammering stopped. It was a roasting hot July afternoon, but Annie had kept her bedroom window closed due to the pounding of jackhammers outside on the street. She put down her history book, got up from the bed and walked over to the window. She was relieved to see that the workers were finished and were preparing to leave for the day. She opened the window to let in some fresh air and went back to her book. As she settled back down onto the bed, she adjusted the chain she wore around her neck, which held a very old family heirloom. The object resembled half an ancient silver medallion and had been left to Annie by her great-grandmother. Annie often speculated as to what the other half might have looked like, wondering if it *too* had a twisted snake around the edge. The ancient medallion had been unearthed by Annie's great-great grandfather, a farmer who had discovered it in one of his fields.

Suddenly, Annie was interrupted by a series of loud bangs. *Surely the construction work isn't starting up again*, she thought. She was about to head back over to the window, when she realized that the sounds were coming from downstairs. When she reached the sitting-room, Annie saw her dad banging on the walls with a hammer. As she watched him, he stopped and put his ear to the wall. Annie called out to him a couple of times, but he was so focused on his task that he didn't seem to hear her.

"Dad!" she yelled at the top of her voice, forcing him to turn around with a start.

Annie's father had been fixing up their house for years, since well before Annie was born. He'd always been convinced that a fireplace was concealed behind one of the walls in the sitting room. Over the years, Annie's mum had tolerated much of the renovation work, debris and dust with increasing protest. Finally, however, she had drawn the line at any further mess, threatening Annie's dad with dire consequences if he so much as touched any of the sitting room walls with his tools.

"Oh, hi, Annie," her dad said. "What are you up to?"

"What are *you* up to?" Annie retorted. "What's going on?"

"Oh this," her dad remarked, holding up the hammer as if it were a historical artifact that required explanation. "I'm looking for that fireplace; you know, the one I'm sure is hidden somewhere in here."

"Yes, I know the one," Annie replied, rolling her eyes. "Isn't that the same fireplace that Mum told you not to bother looking for unless you wanted a whole lot of trouble?"

Her dad smiled.

"Dad, I'm serious," said Annie, firmly. "If Mum finds out what you've been up to, she'll go nuts."

"She'll be fine," her dad replied.

Annie was far from convinced.

"Look," said her dad, "Mum will be shopping until at least five. I'm sure we'll find the fireplace well before she gets back, and then we can quickly clean everything up."

"*We?*" said Annie, arching one eyebrow.

"Come on," her dad smiled mischievously. "You know you want to find it too."

Annie hesitated, then grinned back at him. Much to her mother's dismay, Annie was something of a tomboy and had been eagerly helping her dad ever since she'd been old enough to hold a hammer. She wore her light brown hair short, like a boy, and refused to have her ears pierced or wear anything pink. She only put on feminine clothes when her mother forced her to, for special occasions.

"Give me the other hammer," she said.

Together, they continued searching noisily, each listening carefully for the distinctive sound the hammer would make if it hit something other than solid brickwork. Finally, Annie located a hollow area along the portion of the wall opposite the window.

"Dad," she called out, "there's something here."

Her dad came over and used his hammer to tap on the wall.

"You're right," he said. "Well done, Annie. Now, stand back."

Annie stepped aside and watched as her dad took a deep breath and hit the wall hard with his hammer. It made little impact, except to make an ugly scar on the plasterwork, but when he swung again, three ancient bricks fell inwards.

"It's here!" her dad cheered. "I knew it. Come on, Annie, help me with the rest of the brickwork."

Using her own hammer, Annie joined her dad in knocking out the bricks. But in their excitement and enthusiasm, neither of them paid any attention to the mess they were creating. By the time they had uncovered the whole fireplace, the carpet was covered in debris and the air in the room was thick with white powdery dust from the shattered plaster.

"Mum's not going to like this at all," Annie

said as she surveyed the devastation.

"Well, not like this, anyway," her dad agreed. "Come on. We can admire the fireplace later. Let's get this place cleaned up. I'll make a start if you go and get the vacuum for the carpet."

"Okay," said Annie.

"Hey, that reminds me," her dad said. "I arranged a tour of the archaeological site that you were interested in visiting."

"Really?" exclaimed Annie.

Annie's dad worked for a company financing a new shopping centre in London. When the excavation work began, workers discovered the long forgotten ruins of a medieval abbey. The construction was stopped while a team of archaeologists searched meticulously for ancient artifacts. Annie had studied reports about the discovery and had been pestering her dad for months to arrange a tour of the site.

"Yes," her dad confirmed. "I got a call from Martin Harris, the chief archaeologist, yesterday. You have to be there at eleven o'clock tomorrow."

Chapter Eleven

A Handful of Dust

Martin Harris, the chief archaeologist, was in his early forties, with thick, brown, grey-flecked hair and a full beard. A carpenter's belt, complete with an assortment of tools and a small, bright-yellow radio, hung loosely around his waist.

"The first religious institution on this site was built in the ninth century," he told Annie as they strolled together across the excavation site in the brilliant late morning sunshine.

"Thornbury Abbey was founded in 1132, but was dissolved by Henry VIII during the Reformation in 1539. At that time, the abbey was still in the countryside well outside of London, but over the centuries the city has swallowed it up. We were fortunate to find the ruins when they started work on the shopping centre. We might even solve the mystery, once and for all."

"What mystery?" Annie asked him.

"Thornbury Abbey was rumoured to contain the Heretic's Tomb," Martin replied, "where a woman named Lady Isabella Devereaux had been condemned as a heretic, walled up in a room and left to die of starvation in the mid-fourteenth century."

"That's terrible," exclaimed Annie. "What did she do to deserve that?"

"In 1349," Martin explained, "the Black Death spread through England and claimed over a third of the population before it subsided. Isabella Devereaux lost her entire family to the plague, but somehow she survived. After her family died, she left her home behind and sought refuge in Thornbury Abbey with the nuns."

"So she actually lived here somewhere?" asked Annie, surveying the surrounding ruins.

"She did," Martin confirmed, "although we have no way of knowing if any of the rooms we've found ever belonged to her. Lady Isabella was widely known as a medical pioneer and used her skills to try to cure those suffering from the Black Death. Yet eventually, the church turned against her."

"Why?" Annie asked.

"Accusations were made that she was actually spreading the plague herself somehow, so she was condemned as a witch and walled up in her room to die," Martin continued. "Her chief accuser was Sir Roger de Walsingham. He's buried in a tomb in St. Mary's church, just a few streets away from here."

He pointed into the distance, where Annie could see the distinctive spire of St. Mary's rising into the morning sky.

"Martin," said a female voice coming over the radio on his belt, "are you there?"

"Excuse me," said Martin. As he fumbled to unclip his radio from his belt, he was forced to remove his hammer and flashlight. "Could you hold these for me?"

He handed Annie the hammer and flashlight and spoke into his radio.

"Martin here," he said. "What's up?"

"There's a message for you," the voice said. "It's from head office, and they'd like a call back straight away."

"I'll be right there," Martin replied.

He reattached the radio to his belt and turned to Annie.

"Sorry about this," he apologized, "but I shouldn't be too long. Do you want to explore a little by yourself, then meet me back at the site office in about twenty minutes?"

"Sure," said Annie.

"Most of the artifacts have been cleared away by now," Martin added as he turned to go, "but keep on the marked paths and between the ropes, and you'll be fine."

"See you later," said Annie, as she watched Martin hurry off.

The minute he was out of sight, Annie realized that she still had Martin's hammer and flashlight. Figuring that she would return them to him later, she secured them to her own belt and went off to explore the ruins.

Taking Martin's advice, Annie stuck to the roped-off pathways, not wishing to disturb anything that had not yet been unearthed. The excavation area was covered with trenches and holes, and there were small piles of dirt everywhere. Martin had indicated that most of the significant artifacts had already been cleared away, but there were still men and women dressed in orange vests and white hard hats busy working. Some were examining the half-exposed remnants of a white stone wall, using small brushes to clear away soil and debris. Elsewhere, Annie noted fragments of tiled floors and the remaining stumps of the stone pillars that had once held up the roof of the abbey's substantial church.

The excavation area was encircled by an ugly, bright-blue fence, beyond which Annie could hear the drone of the city traffic. Work on some parts of the shopping centre, along with the associated office development, had continued in the adjacent streets. Huge cranes towered above the excavation area, and Annie could hear the groans of heavy construction equipment.

As she continued exploring, the earth under her feet became unstable. Without warning, she fell several feet through pitch darkness, clattering to the ground with a thump and losing both her shoes in the process. Picking herself up, Annie saw that she was standing inside a long disused fireplace and quickly realized that she must have tumbled down an old chimney shaft. Stepping over the rubble strewn across the hearth, Annie peered into the dark room. She unclipped Martin's flashlight from her belt, switched it on and surveyed her surroundings.

It looked as if there had once been narrow windows set high up on the wall, which were now covered over by earth. Annie saw a bed frame, the straw mattress long since rotted away, and a large wooden trunk. Empty bookshelves filled one wall while other shelves lay broken on the floor beside the splintered wreckage of a piece of furniture that Annie thought might once have been a small cupboard. She recalled how the airtight tombs of ancient Egypt often contained wooden objects that had resisted decay and assumed that this room had been similarly protected. Broken pottery lay scattered everywhere, although a large jug, several small pots and a sturdy looking bowl were undamaged. The room also contained a single table, on which stood a pair of candleholders. On the floor beside it was what looked to be a broken picture frame next to an overturned chair. Annie gasped when she saw a skeleton lying in the dust. Scraps of decayed cloth were still draped over the bones and there was a silver ring on one of the skeleton's fingers.

Annie swallowed her fear and stepped further into the room, stumbling over some pieces of shattered floor tile. In the rubble, she spotted a piece of metal and reached down to pick it up. As Annie wiped off the centuries of dust, the object's strange symbols became familiar. Setting down the flashlight, she held up the family heirloom attached to the chain around her neck and confirmed that it had the same symbols as the metal piece she held in her hand. She put the two halves together, and was amazed to see that they fit together perfectly. It was then a simple matter for Annie to lock them together by fastening the clasp.

Suddenly, a wind began to swirl around the room, scattering dust everywhere. Annie turned to flee and was shocked to see that what had been the fireplace was now a solid wall. She turned around and was horrified to see the skeleton transforming before her eyes. The tattered remnants of material steadily reverted to clothing and the bones themselves began growing flesh and hair, until they turned into the body of a young woman.

chapter Twelve

separated by centuries

Annie backed up against the wall as the woman before her slowly awakened. The broken pottery and wrecked bookshelves still lay on the floor, but the bed frame now had a fresh straw mattress, and the wooden trunk looked relatively new. There were narrow windows clearly visible high on the wall, revealing a full moon and the speckled night sky. On the table, the candleholders now held burning candles.

Annie stared down in disbelief as she realized that only half of the heirloom remained in her hand. Yet curiously, it was neither the old version that she usually wore around her neck, nor the one she had recently found in the rubble. Like the contents of the room, the piece she held in her hand was new.

In the candlelight, Annie could see that the woman had short hair like her own, but was emaciated, with a thin, bony neck and sunken eyes and cheeks. She slowly struggled to her feet and stared at Annie in astonishment.

"Who bistow?" the woman said. *"How comest thow here, trewely?"*

"I'm sorry," said Annie, shaking her head. "I don't understand."

"What seistow?" the woman spoke again, looking extremely confused.

"I don't understand," Annie repeated, beginning to panic. "Where am I?"

The woman didn't attempt to reply again, but instead raised her hand and clicked her fingers twice. She then uttered something that sounded like Latin.

"Audite ut loqui, dicite ut audire possimus."

The woman clicked her fingers again and Annie felt a curious tingling sensation on her tongue and in both ears. She was astounded when she was able to understand the woman's language.

"Can you understand my words now, child?" the woman asked.

"Yes," said Annie, "but how? Where am I?"

The woman smiled and uttered the words, *a nocte in lucem*. Instantly, the candles were extinguished and the room was brightly illuminated, as if they were standing outside in daylight.

"That was a spell to turn night into day within this room," the woman explained. "The words I spoke earlier are an ancient incantation, allowing you to both speak and understand my words. My name is Lady Isabella Devereaux. I have been imprisoned and left to starve here."

"No!" Annie exclaimed. "This can't be happening."

"By the stars!" Isabella declared, once she had taken a good look at Annie's face. "You are the girl that I saw in the mirror."

"The mirror?" said Annie, shaking her head.

"Yes, the mirror that Dominic gave me," Isabella replied. "It allows me to see into the future. I was using it to see if Will was safe, but then it started to show me images from a strange, unfamiliar place with horseless carriages and towering structures. And you were there too."

"I have no idea what you're talking about," said Annie, seriously doubting Isabella's sanity.

Isabella looked down and saw that Annie held half of the amulet in her hands. "This amulet," she said, snatching it from her, "Where did you get it?"

"I don't know," said Annie. "It's different from the one I had before."

Isabella walked over to the corner of the room and lifted up a loose floor tile. "It's gone," she said. "How strange. From how far in the future have you travelled?"

"The future?" said Annie, in bewilderment. "What year is this?"

"It is 1349," Isabella replied

"1349?" Annie gasped. "But that's impossible!"

"I agree," said Isabella, nodding, "but here we are. Somehow, you have journeyed through time itself. Do you recall what happened?"

"I was in this room," Annie replied, "but it was different. I saw something in the dust and picked it up. It looked like the other half of the old medallion my great-grandmother gave me. But when I put the two parts together, I suddenly ended up here."

"I believe I understand," said Isabella. "Just as the amulet has the power to conquer death when it is reassembled, in your hands it has the power to conquer time."

"But how do I get back?" Annie asked, in desperation.

"Get back?" replied Isabella. "I have no idea. The ability to travel through time is far beyond my capability. I had only begun to master a few of the spells and potions in the Book of Vorterius to combat the pestilence."

"The pestilence?" Annie said, feeling very uneasy. "What's that?"

"The plague, the great sickness," said Isabella,

sadly. "So many have died, and so many more are destined to perish."

Annie gulped. She suddenly realized that she was trapped in the time of the Black Death.

"But I can't stay in this place," she said, her voice quivering as she struggled to breathe. "I have to get home."

"Calm down, child," said Isabella, softly. "Now what is your name?"

"Annie."

"Well, Annie," Isabella continued, "this may be beyond my capability, but at least we know that your travelling in time has something to do with the amulet. You say that everything began the instant you put the two halves together and fastened the clasp?"

"So all I need to do is put it back together again?" asked Annie, with renewed hope.

"If only it were so simple," Isabella replied. "We possess only half of the amulet. The other lies in the hands of my assistant, Will, so we are most assuredly trapped in here and destined to starve to death. How did you get in, perchance?"

"I fell down your chimney and into your fireplace," Annie told her. "Maybe we can get out the same way."

"But there is no fireplace in here," countered Isabella.

"It has to be hidden," Annie said, recalling the search with her dad just the day before. She stepped over to the outer wall and ran her fingers across the brickwork. "It must have been covered over before you arrived here."

"But even if it exists," said Isabella, "there is no way for us to access the chimney. The wall is solid as rock."

"We can use this," said Annie, unhooking Martin Harris's hammer from her belt. "Perhaps I can make a gap big enough for us to get through. Then we can climb up the chimney."

"Then let us make haste," said Isabella.

The entire lower level of the abbey was still deserted in accordance with Sir Roger's instructions. Luckily, the wall built over the fireplace was less robust than the one filling the main doorway. Annie used the hammer to smash and remove the stubborn bricks. When she was finished she set it down on the ground and dusted off her hands. Now there was a space large enough for her and Isabella to squeeze through. The inside of the chimney was lit with early dawn light. Annie could see that there were uneven bricks inside the chimney shaft that they could use to escape.

"We can use those bricks as footholds," said Annie. "Ready?"

"Wait a moment," replied Isabella. "We should use the mirror to be certain that we will emerge undetected."

Annie watched Isabella pick up what she had assumed was a broken picture frame.

"The mirror is no more," Isabella sighed. "No matter. If we hurry, we will be long gone before anyone is awake. But you will need to get dressed."

"I'm sorry?" said Annie.

"You will have to cover your strange clothes if we are to remain above suspicion," Isabella pointed out. "I have some items in my trunk that may be to your liking."

Isabella's spare clothing proved to be the wrong size, and dresses weren't exactly Annie's style anyway. However, in the trunk there were also some things belonging to Will. Annie pulled out a plain grey calf-length tunic and black woollen leggings, and when she slipped them on over her t-shirt and jeans, they were a perfect fit. Long black pointed shoes, resembling carpet slippers, completed her outfit. Isabella grabbed a hooded cape and slipped it over her dress. She then slid a thin chain through the hole in the top of the amulet, slipped the chain around her neck and tucked the object inside her clothing.

"Wait," Annie said anxiously, as they prepared to leave. "What about the plague? Isn't it really contagious? I could die out there, couldn't I?"

"The pestilence is very powerful," Isabella confirmed, "but I have something that will protect you."

Isabella poked through the shards of pottery scattered about the floor and spotted a small container that was still intact. She picked it up, dusted off the lid and handed the container to Annie.

"This will provide protection from the disease," she explained, "for the time being at least."

Annie lifted up the lid of the container and stared at the pale yellow liquid inside. "It smells horrible," she said, as she screwed up her nose. "What exactly is this?"

"Do not worry, child, it will not do you any harm," Isabella assured her. "It is a tincture made from crushed herbs and medicinal plants. Swallow it quickly."

Annie seriously doubted that the potion would protect her, but she held her nose and swallowed it.

"We must leave now," said Isabella. "You climb up the chimney first. I will be right behind you."

They emerged on the roof a few feet above the central cloister. Fortunately there was no one around the outside of the abbey. After making the short drop to the ground, Isabella and Annie hurried away toward Thornbury village.

Chapter Thirteen

The Path of the Pestilence

The village was quiet, and Isabella and Annie were able to slip into a barn undetected. Inside the barn, Isabella took a lengthy drink from the fire bucket by the entrance. While she drank, Annie found a wooden box of apples and brought them over to Isabella. As she ate, they made themselves comfortable in the hay and Isabella began telling Annie about her life. She explained how she had lost her family, about Sir Roger's marriage proposal and her decision to live at Thornbury Abbey. She also told Annie that she had worked as a healer, at first by herself and then later with Will, and finally about the wonderful books Dominic had given to her before his death.

"So you used the amulet to cure people?" said Annie, when Isabella had finished.

"No," said Isabella, shaking her head. "Although I knew of its reputed power, I never dared to use it. But Will became very sick as we were returning from the de Walsingham estate. In my distress, I used the amulet to restore his life, but Sir Roger saw what happened. He overheard me say *In nomine Vorterii, mortem expello vitamque restituo* and demanded I give him the amulet."

"What does that mean?" Annie asked her.

"It means in the name of Vorterius, I banish death and restore life," Isabella replied. "I have no idea where the amulet's power comes from, but Will was most assuredly dead and those words brought him back to life. Since I refused to give him the amulet, Sir Roger has wanted me dead. Once he found the books at the abbey he trapped me in my room."

"I've read about the plague in my history books," said Annie. "It's called the Black Death.

In my time, we have hospitals and medicines that can—"

"Please, no more," said Isabella, raising her hand. "As curious as I am about the future, I believe that it would be most unwise for me to possess detailed knowledge of what is to come. I do not wish to risk even more of the Lord's wrath. I may have already been damned for using the amulet of Vorterius to bring Will back to life. I only need to use it once more to transport you back home."

"And to do that we need both halves of the amulet, right?" Annie said.

Isabella nodded.

"I will never allow the amulet to fall into Sir Roger's hands," she said. "I gave one half to Will and hid the other half under the floor tile in my chamber. Once we have used it to send you home, the amulet must be destroyed so that it can never be used for evil."

"So Will has the other half of the amulet?" asked Annie.

"Yes," Isabella replied, "I instructed him to go to my late husband's relatives, who run the White Swan Inn near London Bridge. Before the mirror was destroyed, I saw him working safely as a stable boy, so let us hope that he is still there. Before Sir Roger imprisoned me, I promised Will that I would join him there."

"So we need to get to London," said Annie, standing up.

"A word of warning, Annie," said Isabella, as she got to her feet. "You may be from the future where there are so many wonderful things, I am sure, but you are woefully ignorant of the perils of living in this age. The roads are full of thieves and cutthroats. You must do exactly as I say. Agreed?"

Annie nodded. The horrors of the plague, combined with the possibility of a violent death at the hands of outlaws or being condemned as a witch if anyone discovered who she really was, had her utterly terrified. However, Annie knew that without both halves of the amulet, she would never be able to return to her own time. She had no choice but to accompany Isabella to London.

When they left the barn, Annie was shocked at what she saw. Thornbury was far from the picturesque medieval village she had always imagined from books and movies. The track that ran through the middle of the settlement was a shallow river of mud, with low white-walled houses on either side. Pigs, geese, chickens and stray dogs wandered everywhere, and there was a strong smell of raw sewage in the air.

"What's that?" Annie asked.

Off in the distance, clouds of smoke rose into the sky from one of the nearest fields.

"They are burning the corpses of those who died in the night," Isabella said, with a grimace. "The disease kills people too fast to dig graves for them. Come, it looks as if the blacksmith is leaving his shop to help with the bodies. He will not be gone for long."

Isabella led the way past the back of the houses that lined the main road until they came to the rear of the blacksmith's shop, where four horses stood tethered.

"Wait here," she whispered.

Isabella disappeared inside the shop, returning moments later with a bundle of clothing.

"Now that my hair is short," she explained, "I will need to disguise myself as a man if we are to avoid detection."

Since no one was around, Isabella quickly slipped into the black leggings and thick wool tunic she had found. She then completed her disguise by putting her hooded cloak back on. Once she was finished, she walked over to where the horses were tethered and untied the one with a dapple-grey coat.

"London is at least half a day's ride. This horse should serve us well."

Isabella helped Annie onto the animal's back before climbing up herself. She then jabbed the horse in the ribs with her heels and steered it toward the path at the edge of the forest. Within ten minutes, they were galloping at full speed along the road to London.

chapter fourteen

The streets of London

The ride south to London passed without incident. The road was surprisingly quiet. From the top of the hill leading down to Bishop's Gate, one of seven gates built into the city's fortified walls, Annie marvelled at the medieval London skyline. The buildings were packed tightly together. The tallest structures were the numerous churches, many with impressive spires reaching high into the sky. In the distance, Annie could see the majestic turrets of the Tower of London.

She was amazed at how small medieval London was, a mere fraction of the London she knew. Open fields were clearly visible beyond the houses and shops on either side of the road and past the south bank of the River Thames on the horizon. Bishop's Gate itself was a tall impressive structure built of dull grey stone. Two towers topped with turrets stood on either side of a wide curved archway designed to facilitate the passage of numerous animals and carts filled with goods for the markets. Two smaller arches stood at the bottom of each tower, intended for people on foot. The road through the gate was congested, but eventually Annie and Isabella were able to pass under the archway and ride into the city.

As they made their way along the twisting streets and narrow lanes, Annie was amazed at how far out the upper levels of the houses reached into the street, blocking out the sunlight and making the side alleys dark and forbidding. She had to control the churning in her stomach at the overpowering stench of human and animal waste and rotting refuse. She barely missed being drenched as a woman emptied the contents of her chamber pot onto the street. It was incredibly noisy. Traders shouted from the doorways of shops. Drunks brawled outside overflowing taverns. Stray animals and children ran amok. A man, ringing a bell as he walked, was pushing a cart loaded with bodies. Annie shuddered as he stopped outside a house where a tearful couple carried out the bodies of several children and placed them onto the cart.

Finally, they arrived safely at the White Swan. Isabella brought the horse to a halt but kept a discreet distance from the inn.

"The innkeeper is my late husband's cousin. That is him standing in the stable doorway," she pointed out to Annie. "Go and ask him where we can find Will."

"Me?" said Annie. "Why should I ask him?"

"Because it is too dangerous for me to approach him," Isabella replied. "His family were very kind when they offered me lodgings here, but by now the news about my conviction may have reached the city. I am not altogether convinced that the innkeeper and his family can be trusted to conceal my presence. Do not worry. I will stay out of sight but will keep my eye on you. Just ask him about Will."

Annie dismounted from the horse, which Isabella then guided into a nearby alley from where she could clearly see the White Swan but remain unobserved. Annie cautiously made her way over to the stable entrance, where the innkeeper stood leaning on a shovel, watching the traffic and occasionally greeting passers-by. He was a portly middle-aged man, with an ample belly and rosy cheeks, indicating a fondness for the good food and drink he sold at the inn.

"Excuse me," said Annie as she approached the inn.

"Clear off!" said the man, gruffly. "You brats are always coming in and scaring the horses. Be off with you!"

"I'm looking for someone," she said nervously. "I'm told he works here in the stables."

"John?" the man said. "That good-for-nothing scoundrel from out near Thornbury Abbey? I wish I did know where he was so I could wring his neck."

"So he's not here?" Annie asked.

"No," snapped the man. "He left for the market to get my wife some provisions. But as soon as he got back here, he handed over the fruit and vegetables and left. All he said was that a friend of his was in trouble and that he had to go back to Thornbury. Left me high and dry, he did. Are you a friend of his?"

"Er, no," said Annie. Then thinking quickly she added, "I think I must have the wrong inn. I'm sorry to have troubled you."

"Well then, away with you!" he yelled, as he strode off into the inn. Annie hurried back to where Isabella was waiting.

"He said the stable boy was called John," Annie told her, "but it sounded like Will was using a different name. The innkeeper said that he came from somewhere near Thornbury Abbey and had gone back there to help a friend. That would be you, wouldn't it?"

"I told him to stay here," said Isabella, with an expression of deep concern. "Will shall most certainly forfeit his life if Sir Roger captures him, and the other half of the amulet may be lost to us. We must return to Thornbury immediately. If we leave now perhaps we can reach the village before nightfall."

Isabella helped Annie climb back onto the horse, then they rode off toward Bishop's Gate and the road to Thornbury.

The sun was beginning to set as Isabella and Annie approached the village. At the first sign of houses, Isabella steered the horse into the woods at the side of the road.

"Where are we going?" asked Annie.

"It will not be safe in Thornbury," Isabella replied. "By now the blacksmith will know that his horse has been stolen."

"But we can't stay in the forest, especially at night," Annie protested. "You said that there were outlaws and cutthroats."

"Yes, I did," Isabella agreed, "but even the outlaws stay away from the woods after dark."

"Why?" Annie asked her.

"Because of the wolves," replied Isabella.

"Wolves?" Annie gulped.

"Do not worry," Isabella assured her. "I know a place where we will be safe."

Annie wrapped her arms tightly around Isabella's waist as they rode into the thick forest. It was dusk when they entered a small clearing with a crumbling stone cottage in the centre.

"Is this..." Annie started to ask.

"Yes," said Isabella, anticipating her question as she brought the horse to a halt in front of the cottage. "This was Dominic's home."

She dismounted from the horse and helped Annie to the ground. Annie shuddered at the sight of a small mound of earth topped with heavy stones.

"It looks as if the grave has not been disturbed by the wolves," said Isabella. "We should be safe here tonight."

Isabella eased open the dilapidated door, ushering Annie into the cottage. After tethering the horse, she followed her inside.

"Rest now," Isabella said, "and I will start a fire."

Annie went over to the bare bed and watched as Isabella crouched and began preparing a fire using the sticks and logs that lay scattered around the fire pit.

"Flamma fiat," said Isabella, as she clicked her fingers twice.

Annie was astounded as flames miraculously sprang to life in the centre of the pit.

"There," said Isabella, dusting off her hands and standing up once the fire was crackling. "That should stay alight for a few hours."

Isabella sat down on a small stool beside the bed. Outside a wolf howled in the blackness, startling Annie, who clung tightly to Isabella for protection.

"Fear not," Isabella said softly. "We will be safe, I promise you. It seems like only yesterday that I was here with Dominic. But so much has happened since then. I remember the first time I saw him..."

But Annie fell into a deep sleep and never heard the rest of Isabella's story.

chapter Fifteen

Into the Abbey

It took Will almost an entire day to walk from London to Thornbury Abbey. He kept to the lesser-used side roads whenever he could, suspecting that Sir Roger's spies might be looking for him. Outside the walls of the abbey, three nuns were reading in the shade of the trees and two others walked around in deep prayer. Several women tilled small vegetable patches in the garden, and others were gathering fruit in the orchard. But no one noticed Will slip inside.

Keeping to the perimeter of the central courtyard, Will crept through the silent cloister, then descended into the lower level of the abbey undetected. Stealing along the corridor toward Isabella's room, he heard a sound ahead of him.

Pausing, Will peered cautiously around the corner and saw that the doorway to Isabella's room had been bricked over. A collection of workman's tools lay on the stone floor, and standing before the former entrance was the unmistakable figure of Sir Roger de Walsingham. Will hid in the shadows and watched from a safe distance while Sir Roger removed an eye-level brick from the wall.

Sir Roger de Walsingham gently eased out the brick to take a final, gloating look into the room of Lady Isabella Devereaux. *By now the witch must surely be dead*, he thought to himself. *No one could survive that long without food or water.* When he peered through the hole, however, he was shocked. The room looked much the same as when he had last seen it, except that now the wall covering a concealed fireplace was broken into pieces.

"The sorceress has escaped!" Sir Roger roared with rage. He grabbed a mallet from the floor and began smashing his way through the doorway.

Once he had made a large enough gap, Sir Roger stepped over the rubble and made straight for the fireplace. Peering up the shaft into the gloom, he could clearly see daylight.

"Curse her," he said under his breath.

Lady Isabella was free, and he had no way of knowing exactly when she had escaped. By now she could be miles away. Sir Roger burst out of the room, cursing to himself as he made his way back to the abbey's upper level.

Once Sir Roger was out of sight, Will scampered down the corridor to Isabella's chamber. When he looked inside he was distressed to see the room in complete disarray. And Isabella was gone! She really had been walled up and left to die of starvation, yet the debris in front of the fireplace clearly meant that she had escaped. For a brief moment, Will felt relieved. Yet when he turned to leave he was shocked to find Sir Roger de Walsingham standing right behind him.

His first instinct was to run, but Sir Roger grabbed him tightly by the arm and threw him up against the wall of the corridor with a thud. Swiftly drawing his dagger, Sir Roger pressed the deadly blade up against Will's throat.

"So," sneered Sir Roger, "the witch's apprentice."

He reached out and snatched the amulet fragment from around Will's neck.

"And what have we here?" he said, examining the amulet closely. "This is but a portion of the amulet. Where is the other half?"

Sir Roger pressed the point of the knife into Will's flesh. Will swallowed hard but said nothing, expecting to have his throat slit at any second.

"No matter," Sir Roger said with a cruel grin. "I have ways of loosening your tongue."

chapter sixteen

The Road to Alversham

"Annie, wake up."

Isabella was standing over the bed, smiling down at her. Annie sat up and saw brilliant sunshine outside the cottage's only window.

"I decided to let you sleep while I took the horse down to the stream," said Isabella. "I picked some berries for you."

She gave Annie a handful of wild strawberries, which Annie gladly accepted and ate voraciously.

"Now come," said Isabella, when Annie had finished eating. "We need to go to the abbey."

It was already mid morning when they reached the edge of the forest, just beyond the orchards that bordered Thornbury Abbey. Isabella stopped and dismounted, gesturing for Annie to do the same.

"You will have to go in alone," said Isabella. "I would most surely be recaptured if I accompanied you."

Annie nodded.

"Request to see Abbess Margaret," said Isabella. "Pretend that you are Will's cousin and have just heard that his family died from the plague. Make sure you do not mention my name. Is that clear?"

"Yes," said Annie.

She felt just as nervous as when she had spoken to the innkeeper in London.

"I will wait here for you," Isabella said with a comforting smile. She placed her hand on Annie's shoulder. "God be with you."

Once inside the confines of Thornbury Abbey, Annie entered a wide cloister surrounded by numerous arched passages. In the centre of the cloister stood an ornamental fountain. Annie decided to approach a nun who was filling a small wooden bucket from a basin at its base.

"Forgive me," Annie said as she approached, "but I wish to speak with Abbess Margaret on a matter of some urgency."

"The abbess?" said the nun, frowning. "I am afraid the abbess is far too busy to concern herself with children. Run along now."

"But I am Will's cousin," said Annie. "My family only recently heard of his terrible tragedy, and we were told that he was living here at the abbey."

"The boy who was Lady Isabella's assistant?" asked the nun, with a look of surprise. "Come with me at once, child. The abbess will be most anxious to meet you."

Abbess Margaret sat in an ornately carved chair behind a wide wooden table on which lay a small pile of books and several scrolls bound with coloured ribbon. On the wall behind her hung a collection of keys in all shapes and sizes.

"Please be seated, child," the abbess said with a smile, gesturing to a chair in front of the table.

Annie sat down, and the abbess spoke again.

"I am sorry to be the bearer of sad tidings," she said, with an expression of deep concern. "Your cousin Will was indeed living with us here at the abbey, but now I fear for his life."

Annie listened calmly as Abbess Margaret told her what had happened.

"So where is Will now?" Annie asked, when the abbess had finished.

"Sir Roger was here last night," said the abbess. "He detained young Will and took him to his castle at Alversham. Sir Roger is a powerful and ruthless man. Please believe me when I say that he would have killed me without a second thought if I had opposed him."

"Thank you for telling me this," Annie said, as she stood up and prepared to leave.

"Where will you go, my child?" asked the abbess.

"I will return to my family and inform them of

what has happened," Annie replied. "Perhaps we can petition Sir Roger to release Will."

"A noble intention," said the abbess, nodding, "but I doubt if Sir Roger will pay much attention. May God be with you."

Annie returned to where Isabella was waiting at the edge of the forest and explained what had happened.

"It is as I feared," Isabella said gravely. "Sir Roger knows that I have escaped, and he now has Will. He no doubt assumes that I have the amulet's other half."

"So what do we do now?" asked Annie.

"We must ride to Alversham Castle," Isabella replied. "It will be safer if we travel through the woods. Sir Roger's men will not think to look for us there."

When they were close to the castle, Isabella came to a halt and tied the horse to a tree. She and Annie then crept through the bushes and shrubs to the top of a ridge overlooking Sir Roger de Walsingham's stronghold.

Alversham Castle was constructed of dark grey weathered stone and had four colossal rounded towers topped with turrets at each corner, while the keep in the centre of the main courtyard boasted two square towers. The fortress was well-protected by a wide moat and a formidable gatehouse. Black flags displaying the de Walsingham family's white stag emblem fluttered from the battlements, and guards dressed in black chainmail stood on the castle ramparts, anxiously scanning the surrounding countryside. Soldiers and horses pulling wagons clattered across the drawbridge, which was suspended from the castle walls by thick iron chains.

"It appears that the stories are true," Isabella muttered to herself.

"What do you mean?" Annie asked her.

"Each lord is expected to maintain his own army," Isabella explained, pointing to the traffic crossing the moat, "but this is excessive. There are rumours that Sir Roger has been stockpiling weapons and supplies for an insurrection against the king."

"Is that Sir Roger?" Annie asked, pointing to a stocky, muscular man who appeared to be giving orders.

"No," replied Isabella, "that is Fitzwalter, Sir Roger's ruthless henchman. It would appear that Sir Roger's plans are close to fruition."

"What should we do?" asked Annie.

"We must inform the sheriff, Sir Edmund Courteney, of Sir Roger's treason."

"But what about Will?" Annie asked. "We have to save him."

"You are right," sighed Isabella. "But to rescue Will we need Sir Edmund's help. Besides, we must stop Sir Roger from executing his plans. Courteney Manor is not that far from here. We will be back well before nightfall."

"But Will could be dead by then," Annie protested. "We have to get in there *now*."

"It is too dangerous," said Isabella, shaking her head. "There are too many soldiers. We need to secure Sir Edmund's assistance first."

"Then why don't you go on your own?" Annie suggested. "I can hide myself in one of the wagons before it's driven inside the main gate. I'll be able to find Will, if he's still alive."

Isabella thought hard for a moment.

"So be it," she reluctantly agreed. "You will be in grave danger, but you will have a better chance of success if you go alone."

"They will be looking for you," Annie warned as Isabella climbed up onto the horse. "Be careful."

"I will," promised Isabella. "Take care, Annie. I will return as swiftly as I can."

After watching Isabella disappear into the woods, Annie clambered over the ridge and crept down the slope to the road, where several wagons were lined up. Men were standing around chatting as they waited for the guards at the main gate to signal that they could approach the castle. Crouching low, Annie selected an unattended wagon, climbed up using the spokes of the wheel as footholds and slid under the rough sackcloth.

chapter seventeen

Resurrection for insurrection

Inside the great hall of Alversham Castle, Will sat in a chair beside a decorated stone fireplace, while Sir Roger de Walsingham paced the floor in front of him. The hall had only one exit, which was securely barred by the solid frame of Fitzwalter. Beneath the braces and beams of the wide, open-timbered ceiling, sunlight shimmered through high arched windows. On one wall hung a tapestry depicting knights in gleaming armour, parading on horseback at a tournament whose grounds were filled with tents of red, green and gold. Opposite, another tapestry showed a wild boar in a thickly forested landscape. All around the room, there were shields and other regalia displaying the de Walsingham family crest.

"It is remarkable, is it not," said Sir Roger, as he stood directly in front of the chair, staring at the amulet fragment in the palm of his hand, "that something so plain, so simple, could possess such immense power."

"Power, my lord?" Will replied, innocently. "I know only that my mistress gave me the object for safekeeping. I believe it is a talisman of some sort, to assist her in her work. Is it your intention to become a healer yourself?"

"A healer?" cackled Sir Roger. "Well, in a manner of speaking. I intend to use the power of the amulet to raise an army of the dead and seize the kingdom—with your help, of course."

"My lord?" said Will.

"The instructions regarding the forging of the amulet are missing," Sir Roger continued, "but my alchemist, Skerne, has been hard at work on the pagan text and has created an identical amulet. He has, unfortunately, been unable to endow it with any powers, but now at least we have half of the original. Combined with Skerne's, I may yet obtain the power of life over death. I am sure that you are aware of the words *mortis victor* and *vitae restitutor*?"

"I know nothing of such matters, my lord," Will said.

"Liar!" screeched Sir Roger.

With the back of his hand, he slapped Will hard across the face, knocking him off the chair and sending him sprawling toward the fireplace.

"Your mistress destroyed or has hidden the instructions that make the amulet work," continued Sir Roger. "I saw her bring you back to life. The Latin verse that revived you is all that I need."

"My lord," protested Will, cowering on the cold stone floor, "I swear to you that I am ignorant of such things."

"We shall see," said Sir Roger, with a twisted smile. "I doubt if even Lady Isabella will be able to heal you once Skerne is finished with you."

He pulled Will to his feet and dragged him roughly toward the exit.

"Tell the riders to make ready," Sir Roger ordered Fitzwalter. "The scrolls that signal the beginning of the rebellion are in my private quarters. You know what to do."

Fitzwalter nodded and hurried off down the hallway, while Sir Roger dragged Will down the dark staircase to Skerne's laboratory.

chapter Eighteen

within the walls

As the wagon rumbled across the drawbridge and past the guards into the interior of Alversham Castle, Annie peered out from under the sackcloth. Above the main gate was a raised portcullis, its menacing spikes pointing downward. Annie knew that the gate would swiftly descend if the castle were attacked, and she hoped she would be able to locate Will before they were both trapped inside.

The wagon came to a halt in the central courtyard, which was crammed with military equipment and bustling with horses and soldiers wearing the de Walsingham crest. On the surrounding walls, wooden staircases led up to the parapets, where heavily armed men stood ready to repel any assault. The keep in the centre of the courtyard was usually where the lord of the manor had his private quarters, and Annie guessed that was where Will was most likely being held. After checking that the coast was clear, she began climbing out of the wagon. However, she was forced to duck back under the sackcloth when Fitzwalter emerged from the keep's entrance and beckoned to one of the soldiers before heading in her direction. Annie's heart pounded as the two men stood right beside the wagon where she was concealed.

"Is the boy dead, then?" the soldier asked matter-of-factly.

"Lord de Walsingham has taken him down to Skerne's laboratory," replied Fitzwalter. "He will not come out alive. Are your men ready for battle?"

"Almost," the soldier replied. "We have but a few final arrangements."

"Good," said Fitzwalter. "Our allies will rise up simultaneously as soon as they receive our signal."

Through a tiny hole in the cloth, Annie saw Fitzwalter pointing to the tallest window in the rear tower of the keep.

"You may collect the letters from my lord's apartments," Fitzwalter continued. "Give them to your swiftest riders as soon as you have finished making your preparations."

The two men went their separate ways, and once Annie was convinced she was alone she emerged into the daylight. Quickly dropping down from the wagon, she took cover behind the enormous wooden wheel of a catapult, then darted the short distance into the keep.

When she was safely inside the entrance, Annie caught her breath in the darkened corridor. To her right there was a winding staircase that led to the upper reaches of the tower, where Fitzwalter had indicated that Sir Roger's living quarters were situated. To her left, a more daunting set of stairs descended into the gloom, presumably in the direction of Skerne's laboratory. Annie wasn't sure what to do. She thought that there might be a chance to thwart Sir Roger's plans, if she stole the letters before they were dispatched to his fellow conspirators. Isabella would then have evidence to present to Sir Edmund Courteney in case he didn't believe her story. Steeling herself for the task ahead, Annie resolved to grab Sir Roger's letters and then brave the terrors of Skerne's laboratory.

She cautiously climbed the winding staircase to the uppermost level and was relieved to discover that Sir Roger's private quarters were unguarded. Darting across the landing, Annie gently eased the door open. Inside she saw a large canopy bed with its linen hangings pulled back. Next to the bed, a lamp hung from an iron ring.

Annie spotted a collection of scrolls on a small table. She moved swiftly across the room and saw that they were sealed with the de Walsingham family crest. Snatching the scrolls, she raced out of the room and hurried back down the staircase. But when she reached the bottom, she realized in horror that she was not alone.

chapter Nineteen

skerne's lair

Sir Roger never once relaxed his grip as he escorted Will down the murky staircase to where Skerne was waiting. Opening the door to the laboratory, Sir Roger stepped inside, dragging Will after him. The dingy room was shrouded in shadows, and white-hot coals smouldered in the fireplace. In a chair beside the hearth, a man with bedraggled shoulder-length grey hair sat poring over a book.

"Skerne," Sir Roger called out as he dragged Will over to the table.

"Is this the boy?" Skerne asked, getting up from his seat and hobbling over to meet them.

"Yes," said Sir Roger, tossing Skerne the half amulet and its chain. "And this is the object he was carrying. See what you can do with it, and determine the verse to unlock its powers. I do not care what you have to do, but get him to talk! Do you understand?"

"Perfectly, my lord," Skerne answered, his grin exposing his many missing teeth.

"I have urgent matters to discuss with Fitzwalter," said Sir Roger, turning to leave, "but I wish to be informed the moment you have the incantation."

"Yes, my lord," Skerne replied.

Sir Roger strode out of the laboratory and slammed the door. Skerne took a key from his pocket and locked it. Grabbing Will by the arm, Skerne pulled him over to the table.

"So you are Lady Isabella's assistant," he said as he slipped the chain holding the half amulet around his own neck.

"I am," Will declared.

"If you helped her with her healing work, I am sure you are also familiar with this."

He grabbed the Book of Vorterius from the table and showed Will the cover.

"I have seen that book before," Will admitted.

"So you also know what the amulet is capable of when it is assembled," said Skerne. "My master has informed me that you were restored to life. Is that true?"

"I am told that I was," said Will, evasively. "But I have no idea how."

"Do not take me for a fool, boy," Skerne snarled. "You must be well aware that the amulet draws poison from the body and into itself, restoring the person to life. Your mistress took great care to hide the most important information in this book. I have been able to forge an identical amulet here in my laboratory, but the incantation that makes it work has remained elusive."

"I know nothing of such things," said Will.

"Well, I think that you do," Skerne responded menacingly." Now, will you tell me the words needed to unlock the amulet's power freely, or do I need to be more persuasive?"

Skerne reached down to the hearth and picked up a long iron rod, which glowed white-hot from the fire. Will was terrified. His mind raced as he desperately scanned the room for a way out. There was only one door to the laboratory, and it was locked. What he needed was a diversion.

"Wait," he said. "I will do as you ask. Lady Isabella has abandoned me anyway."

"A most wise choice," Skerne replied as he replaced the rod in the hearth. "Since we have only one half of the original amulet, perhaps it will work if I combine it with half of the amulet I made."

Skerne walked over to a small table against the wall and returned with half an amulet, which he fitted together with Will's.

"And now, boy," he said, "the incantation."

"I will need to study the text, to be sure," said Will, still trying to gain time.

"Don't try to stall," Skerne snarled. "The spell has been removed from the book. I have searched it from cover to cover, over and over again."

Will was faced with an impossible choice. To tell Skerne the spell would enable Sir Roger to raise an unholy army of the dead. Yet if he refused, Skerne would torture him until he revealed it. Suddenly, a plan came to mind. Will decided to recite the verse backwards, suspecting that Skerne would not know the difference. Will hoped that the alchemist's delight would throw him off guard long enough for Will to overpower him, grab the key and escape.

"Well?" said Skerne, impatiently.

"The words you need," Will told him, "are *restituo vitamque expello mortem Vorterii nomine in.*"

"My thanks to you, boy," replied Skerne, with a cruel smirk. "As a reward, I will ensure that your death is swift and painless."

After fastening the clasp securely, Skerne repeated the words that Will had spoken to him, and the amulet glowed pale green. Will was astonished at what he saw. The instant Skerne mouthed the final word of the reversed incantation, the plague's unmistakable blotches began appearing all over his hands and face.

"No!" yelled Skerne in horror as the grotesque blemishes consumed his skin. Stepping back, Will realized what was happening. Within seconds,

Skerne's face was scarcely recognizable beneath a multitude of sores. Skerne then began rapidly aging before Will's eyes. The alchemist screamed in agony as his flesh quickly wasted away. He tried to grab Will, but it was too late, and he turned into a skeleton and collapsed in a pile of bones on the floor.

Once Will had recovered his composure, he cautiously approached Skerne's skeletal remains and picked up the amulet. After unfastening the clasp and removing the portion Skerne had forged, Will slipped the chain around his neck. He then reached into the pocket of the alchemist's tunic and pulled out the key. He picked up the Book of Vorterius and a small dagger from the side table, unlocked the door and raced out of the laboratory.

chapter Twenty

The Reckoning

With the Book of Vorterius in one hand and the dagger held tightly in the other, Will scrambled up the darkened staircase to the surface. When he entered the hallway, he was startled by someone running down the stairs from the upper level. It was a girl around his age, carrying some scrolls.

"Who are you?" Will demanded, brandishing the dagger menacingly and forcing the girl to back up against the wall.

"My name is Annie," she said quickly. "I'm a friend of Lady Isabella."

"How do I know that?" said Will. "For all I know you could be working for de Walsingham."

"I heard about your work healing the sick," Annie gasped.

"That is common knowledge," said Will, dismissively.

"I know that you were dead," Annie said, "and that Isabella was able to revive you."

Will thought for a moment. As he examined Annie closer he realized that her tunic looked familiar.

"Sir Roger knew that," he retorted, "and so did Skerne. Maybe Fitzwalter too and even some of the soldiers. It proves nothing."

"But I know the words she used to restore your life," Annie exclaimed, in desperation.

"Do you?" he said skeptically. He moved the blade closer to Annie's throat. "Then what were they?"

Annie gulped, hoping desperately that she could remember the verse correctly.

"*In nomine Vorterii, mortem expello vitamque restituo*," she said.

"You do indeed speak the truth," said Will, lowering the dagger. "Only Lady Isabella and I know the incantation. What are those scrolls you are carrying?"

"These letters were to be delivered to Sir Roger's accomplices in his plan to seize the kingdom," Annie explained. "Is that the Book of Vorterius?"

"Yes," said Will.

"Do you still have half of the amulet?" asked Annie.

"I do," Will confirmed, lifting up the chain and showing Annie the amulet portion. "I assume the other half is safe?"

Before Annie could respond, she was interrupted by the shouts of soldiers and the sounds of battle coming from the direction of the main courtyard.

"What was that?" asked Will.

"Lady Isabella went to get help from Sir Edmund Courteney," Annie replied. "Probably his men are storming the castle. We'd better find somewhere to hide."

As they turned to go, Sir Roger de Walsingham barred their way, his sword drawn.

"You may have slipped away from Skerne," he snarled, "but you will not escape me so easily. And who is this? Another of Lady Isabella's helpers?"

Annie and Will backed away into the great hall.

"Courteney is here with his men," growled Sir Roger, advancing toward them. "Did you send a message to him, boy? Or perhaps it was your friend here?"

When Annie and Will reached the huge fireplace, they could go no further. Sir Roger snatched the half amulet from around Will's neck and placed it around his own. He raised his sword and was about to strike, but shouting interrupted him.

"De Walsingham!"

Sir Roger whirled around to see Sir Edmund Courteney and Isabella standing in the doorway. Annie and Will broke away from Sir Roger and raced across the great hall toward them. Courteney stepped into the hall, followed by his men, who began to fan out along the walls.

"We have already arrested Fitzwalter," Courteney said calmly, "and your soldiers are either dead or in custody, as you soon will be."

"By what right do you invade my estate, Courteney?" Sir Roger demanded.

"By my right as sheriff to arrest those who are guilty of crimes," Courteney replied. "Crimes such as treason and heresy."

"Heresy?" said Sir Roger, mockingly. "That witch beside you is a *convicted* heretic, as well you know."

"I know only of your false accusations against Lady Isabella," Courteney shot back, "and that it is you who are truly engaged in witchcraft."

"You dare to accuse me!" Sir Roger barked. "I know what you seek. The Courteneys have coveted the de Walsingham lands for centuries, but your plan will fail! You have no evidence linking me to sorcery."

"My lord," said Will, "I found this book about the black arts in Skerne's laboratory."

He handed the Book of Vorterius to Courteney, who opened it and flipped through the pages.

"What do you say to this, de Walsingham?" Courteney asked, holding up the book.

"Am I to be held responsible for the actions of my servants?" Sir Roger scathingly replied. "Skerne has many books. Am I expected to be familiar with all of them?"

"And why have you been stockpiling weapons and recruiting soldiers?" Courteney pressed him. "Such strength of arms is more than sufficient to challenge the king himself. Perhaps that is your intention?"

"Speculation," scoffed Sir Roger. "Nothing more."

Annie then handed one of the scrolls to Courteney, who unrolled it and quickly scanned the contents.

"These letters bearing your seal say otherwise," he said. "I am sure I do not need to remind you, Sir Roger, of the punishment for treason. You may surrender willingly or my men will take you by force."

"Never!" roared Sir Roger.

Raising his sword high over his head, Sir Roger charged directly at Courteney but was easily overwhelmed. Four of Courteney's men subdued

Sir Roger. Then they secured his arms with rope and dragged him screaming out of the hall.

"Just a moment," said Isabella, as they reached the doorway. "He has something that belongs to me."

With a smile, she took the half amulet from Sir Roger's neck and placed it around her own.

"You witch!" yelled Sir Roger. "Courteney, you must believe me. She is the servant of Satan! The amulet is magic. It has the power to conquer death itself!"

"Such wild accusations only serve to confirm his guilt," Isabella said to Courteney. "Sir Roger is clearly possessed, as well as being both a heretic and a traitor."

"Take him away," ordered Courteney, handing Isabella the Book of Vorterius.

Once his men had taken the still ranting Sir Roger out into the courtyard, Courteney turned to Will.

"Bring those letters, Will. I will need them to inform the sheriffs in other parts of the kingdom of Sir Roger's plot."

"Yes, my lord," said Will.

"Lady Isabella," Courteney added, "if you would also bring the book of enchantments."

"Perhaps it would be best if it is immediately destroyed?"

"As you wish," Courteney nodded and left the hall to join his men.

"My lady," said Will. "Skerne has forged a duplicate amulet."

"As I suspected. I shall be sure to destroy it."

Through the window, Isabella and Annie watched as Will joined Courteney and his men on the far side of the castle courtyard. Then Isabella took the Book of Vorterius over to the fireplace.

"What are you going to do?" Annie asked her.

"The Book of Vorterius must be destroyed," Isabella informed her. "It is too powerful for anyone to possess, no matter how noble their intentions."

She threw it into the fireplace.

"Stand back," she said to Annie, then with two clicks of her fingers said, *"Flamma fiat!"*

The fireplace suddenly erupted in flames, and in seconds the Book of Vorterius was reduced to a pile of ash.

"And now," Isabella said, "it is time for you to return home. Do you remember what you did when you first found the amulet?"

"I think so," said Annie. "I put both halves together out of curiosity, but nothing happened until I fastened the clasp."

"Then that is what you must do again," said Isabella.

Taking her half of the amulet, she joined it to Will's portion but left the clasp open. She then handed the amulet to Annie.

"Goodbye, Annie," she said. "I owe you my life."

"But what will happen to you now?" Annie asked her. "Are you still in danger?"

"Sir Edmund has overturned my conviction," Isabella replied, with a smile, "and has promised to look after Will and me. Have no fear."

After quickly embracing her, Isabella stepped away from the fireplace. Annie then fastened the clasp together and vanished.

That evening, bathed in the glow of flaming torches in the depths of Thornbury Abbey, Sir Edmund Courteney and Abbess Margaret watched as the wall covering the doorway of Isabella's former chamber was rebuilt. Inside the room, Sir Roger de Walsingham, newly convicted as a heretic, awoke from his sleeping draught and screamed in rage as the final brick was inserted, condemning him to a slow and agonizing death.

chapter Twenty-one

The Heretic's Tomb

Annie found herself back in her own time, standing on the hearth in front of the fireplace in Isabella's room. The amulet was still in one piece, attached to the chain around her neck, but now both halves, along with the clasp, had assumed an ancient weathered appearance. In the rubble, Annie saw Martin's flashlight, still switched on, and was also relieved to see her shoes that had fallen off when she tumbled down the chimney.

Using the flashlight to examine the darkened room, Annie noted that the narrow windows high up on the wall were now once again covered by earth. However, the wooden trunk, the bookshelves, the shattered remains of Isabella's cabinet and all the pottery, whether broken or intact, were missing. Yet the bed-frame was still present, as were the table and chair, and on the floor, a skeleton lay in the dust. Oddly however, the bones had no remnants of cloth, and there were no rings on any of the skeleton's fingers. Annie was about to go and take a closer look, when she heard a voice from above.

"Annie? Are you down there?"

It was Martin Harris.

"Yes," Annie called back.

As he started to clamber down the chimney, Annie quickly removed Will's clothes and shoes, hiding them in the pile of rubble at the side of the fireplace, and slipped into her own shoes. She looked down and to her amazement saw Martin's hammer, now covered in centuries of rust. She reached to pick it up, but the hammer disintegrated in her hand.

"There you are," said Martin, as he stumbled into the room. "I wondered what happened to you. Are you okay?"

He then spotted the skeleton lying in the corner, and his eyes widened in astonishment.

"This is incredible," he exclaimed, "simply incredible. After all our work here at the site, you've actually found the Heretic's Tomb, the final resting-place of Sir Roger de Walsingham."

"I'm sorry," said Annie, "who did you say?"

"Sir Roger de Walsingham," Martin repeated. "You remember that I told you earlier how he was condemned as a heretic, walled up in a room and left to die of starvation in the time of the Black Death? Forbidden books about black magic were found at his castle, and he was suspected of planning a rebellion against King Edward III. Thornbury Abbey was rumoured to be the location where he died. It became known as the Heretic's Tomb. This discovery could extend the dig for months. I have to let my team know. Come on. I'll take you back up to the surface."

With a final glance at the skeleton of Sir Roger de Walsingham, Annie followed Martin into the fireplace and climbed up the chimney behind him.

On the surface, while Martin excitedly contacted his colleagues with his radio, Annie thought about what had happened. By going back into the past and rescuing Isabella and Will, she had altered the former chain of events. Sir Roger had been condemned as a heretic in Isabella's place and had been walled up in the room to die.

But what happened to Isabella and Will? she wondered.

"Are you okay?" Martin asked her, as he finished his call.

"I'm fine," replied Annie.

"Are you sure?" Martin pressed her. "You look a little pale."

"I'm just tired, that's all," said Annie.

"Maybe you should head home," Martin suggested. "I have to cut our tour short anyway, now that this has come to light.

"I think I read somewhere that a Lady Isabella Devereaux once lived in Thornbury Abbey," Annie said.

"I'm not familiar with that last name," said Martin, "but I think there's a Lady Isabella buried in St. Mary's church, just a few streets away. Maybe that's who you were thinking of?"

"Yes," Annie said, "you're probably right. I'll go and check it out on the way home. Thanks for the tour."

"You're very welcome, Annie," said Martin. "I'll be sure to invite you back when I have some more time, I promise."

Annie left the excavation site and made the short journey to St. Mary's Church, which had been built a generation after the time of the Black Death. Like Thornbury Abbey, it had stood in the heart of the countryside in the Middle Ages but had long since been swallowed up by the city. St. Mary's was an imposing stone structure surrounded by a churchyard filled with green lawns, mature trees and park benches. The clock-tower and steeple were topped with a spire rising proudly above the adjacent modern office buildings. Annie crossed the street and hurried up the pathway to the church's main entrance. Just inside the door, a woman was straightening the books and postcards in the racks of a small gift shop.

"Good afternoon," she said. "Welcome to St. Mary's. Can I interest you in a guide book?"

"Actually, I'm just here to see the tomb," said Annie.

"Well, there are several here in the church," the woman replied. "Were you looking for any in particular?"

"Yes," said Annie. "I think her name was Lady Isabella."

"Ah yes," the woman answered, with a smile. "You'll find that one, along with the rest of her family, in the Holy Cross Chapel at the far end."

"Thank you," said Annie.

She left the gift shop and entered the main body of the church. The nave was flanked by row upon row of dark wooden pews and thick stone columns, all joined by high pointed arches. Behind the main altar were three extremely long pointed windows, beautifully decorated with coloured stained glass. Above them was an even larger circular window depicting religious figures. When Annie reached the ornately carved wooden pulpit at the end of the nave, she followed the arrow pointing toward the Holy Cross Chapel.

Inside the chapel, Annie saw the double tomb of a man and a woman lying side by side. The hands of the marble effigies were pressed together in prayer. As she approached the tomb, she was astonished to see that the carved letters beneath the figure of the woman read *Lady Isabella Courteney*. Moving closer, Annie examined the face of the female figure in more detail. The face bore a remarkable resemblance to the Lady Isabella whom Annie had known. Beside her lay the effigy of Sir Edmund Courteney. Annie edged closer to read the small brass plaque at their feet.

Here lie the remains of Sir Edmund Courteney (1313 to 1372), his second wife Lady Isabella (1324 to 1396), their four children, Robert, Thomas, Ann, Eleanor and their adopted son William. Sir Edmund was a loyal servant of King Edward III and sheriff of the county. Lady Isabella Courteney was renowned as an early medical pioneer during the Black Death and during subsequent outbreaks of the plague for the remainder of the fourteenth century.

Annie smiled to herself as she gazed again at the marble face of Lady Isabella. She had married Sir Edmund, had another family and even adopted Will. Reaching out to touch the cold fingers of Lady Isabella's memorial, Annie whispered, "Goodbye."

That night, Annie lay on her bed thinking about her incredible adventure into the past. She held the amulet in her hand, wondering if the object's power was gone forever.

"Hey, Annie," said her dad, as he stood in the doorway. "Are you still up? It's very late."

"Oh, hi, Dad," Annie replied. "How did Mum take the news about the new fireplace?"

"Surprisingly well," said her dad, with a chuckle. "As long as I finish it off she won't stay mad at me for too long. What do you have there?"

"I saw this thing in the dirt at the site," said Annie, holding up the amulet. "It turned out to be an exact fit to great-great-granddad's old coin."

"That's pretty amazing," said her dad. "What did Martin have to say?"

"Not too much," Annie replied, more or less truthfully. "He was too preoccupied with a new burial chamber they'd just found."

"Really?" said her dad, sounding disappointed. "I guess that'll delay the shopping centre even more. So how was your tour of the excavation site?"

"Interesting," Annie replied, with a wry smile. "Very interesting."